D0475454

HAM-LET™

A SHAKESPEAREAN MASH-UP

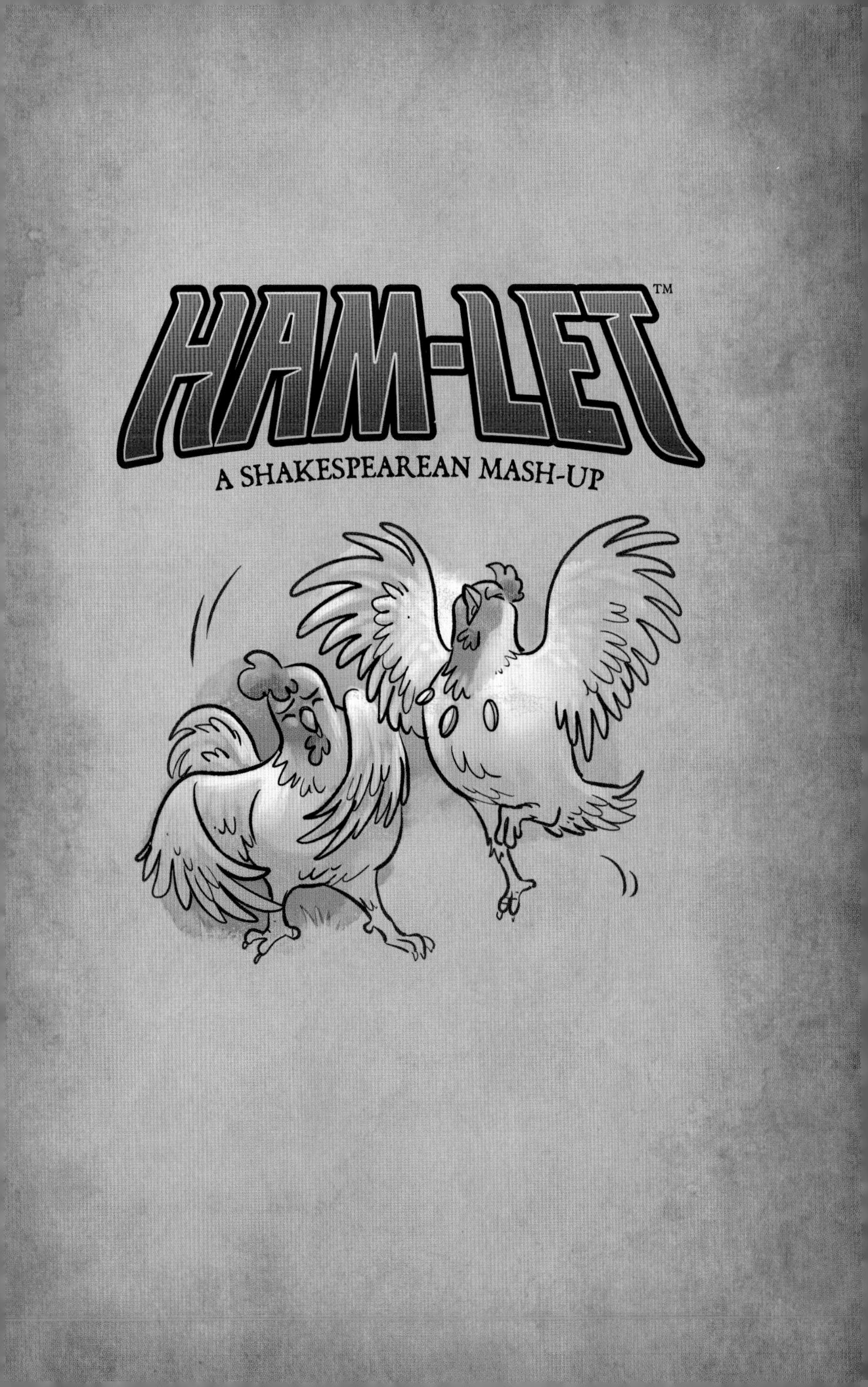

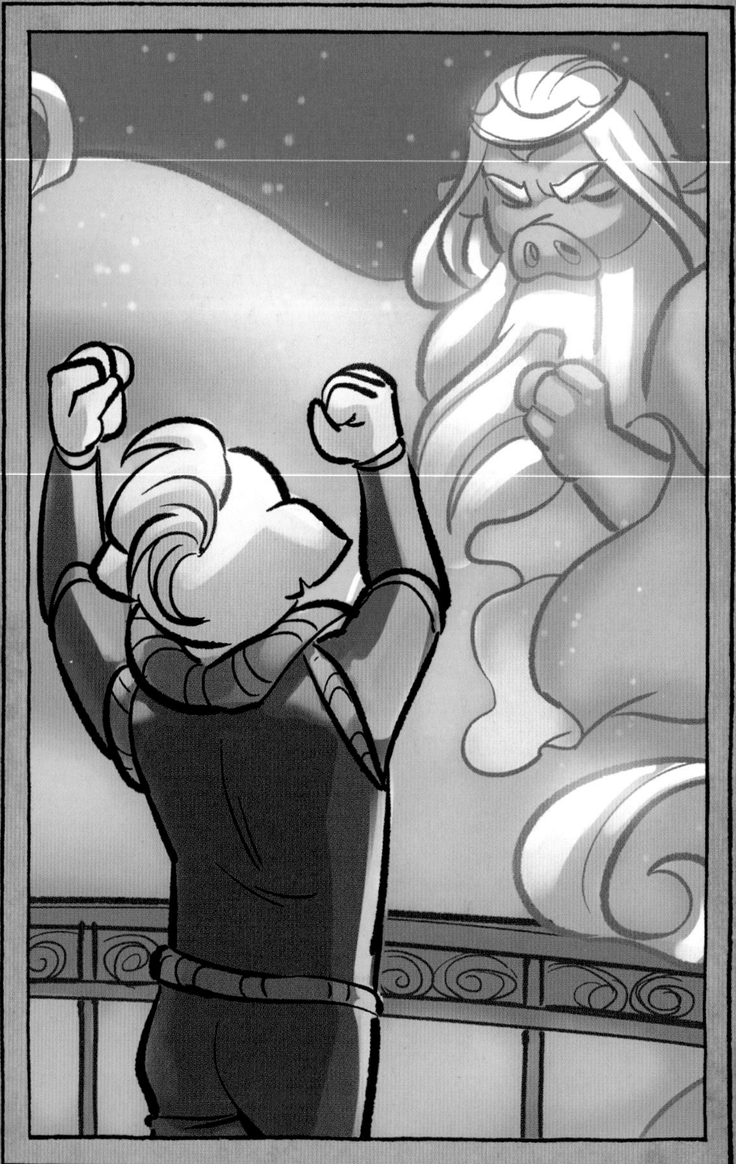

HAM-LET ™

A SHAKESPEAREAN MASH-UP

SCRIPT
Jim Burnstein & Garrett Schiff

COVER & LINE ART
Elisa Ferrari

COLORS
Valerio Alloro

LETTERS
Frank Cvetkovic

DARK HORSE BOOKS

PRESIDENT & PUBLISHER Mike Richardson

EDITOR Megan Walker

COLLECTION DESIGNER Diego Morales-Portillo

DIGITAL ART TECHNICIAN Betsy Howitt

Published by Dark Horse Books
A division of Dark Horse Comics LLC
10956 SE Main Street, Milwaukie, OR 97222

DarkHorse.com

International Licensing: (503) 905-2377

To find a comics shop in your area, visit comicshoplocator.com

First edition: March 2022
Ebook ISBN 978-1-50672-090-6   ◆   Hardcover ISBN 978-1-50672-089-0

1 3 5 7 9 10 8 6 4 2
Printed in China

Library of Congress Cataloging-in-Publication Data

Names: Burnstein, Jim, writer. | Schiff, Garrett K., writer. | Ferrari,
    Elisa, 1988- artist. | Alloro, Valerio, colourist. | Cvetkovic, Frank,
    letterer.
Title: Ham-let : a Shakespearean mash-up / writers, Jim Burnstein, Garrett
    Schiff ; interior and cover art, Elisa Ferrari ; colors, Valerio Alloro
    ; letters, Frank Cvetkovic.
Description: Milwaukie, OR : Dark Horse Books, [2022]
Identifiers: LCCN 2021039513 | ISBN 9781506720890 (hardcover) | ISBN
    9781506720906 (ebook)
Subjects: CYAC: Graphic novels. | Pigs--Fiction. | Princes--Fiction. |
    Betrayal--Fiction. | LCGFT: Funny animal comics. | Graphic novels.
Classification: LCC PZ7.7.B894 Ham 2022 | DDC 741.5/973--dc23
LC record available at https://lccn.loc.gov/2021039513

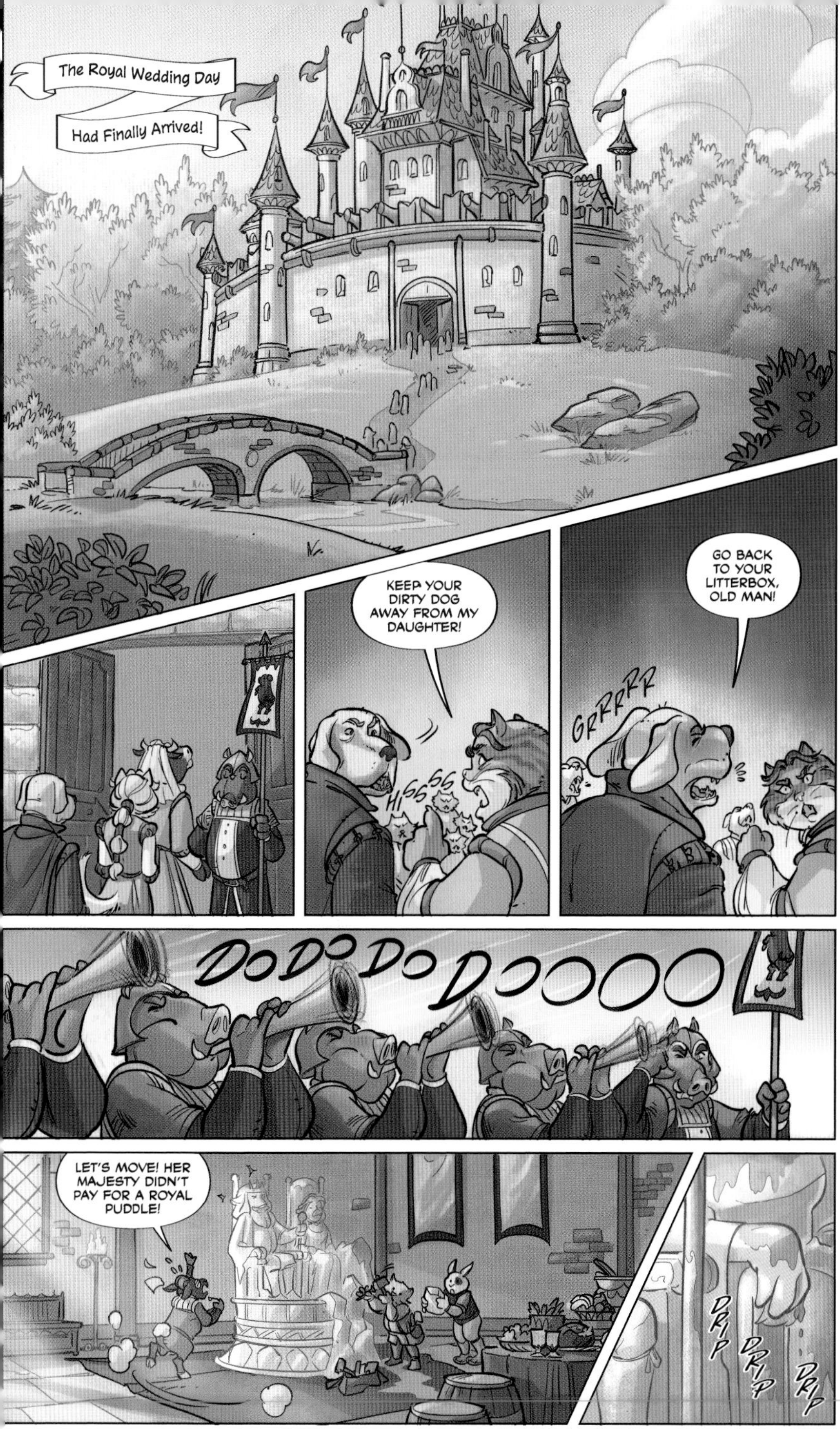
The Royal Wedding Day
Had Finally Arrived!
KEEP YOUR DIRTY DOG AWAY FROM MY DAUGHTER!
HISSSS
GO BACK TO YOUR LITTERBOX, OLD MAN!
GRRRRR
DODODO DOOOOO
LET'S MOVE! HER MAJESTY DIDN'T PAY FOR A ROYAL PUDDLE!
DRIP
DRIP
DRIP

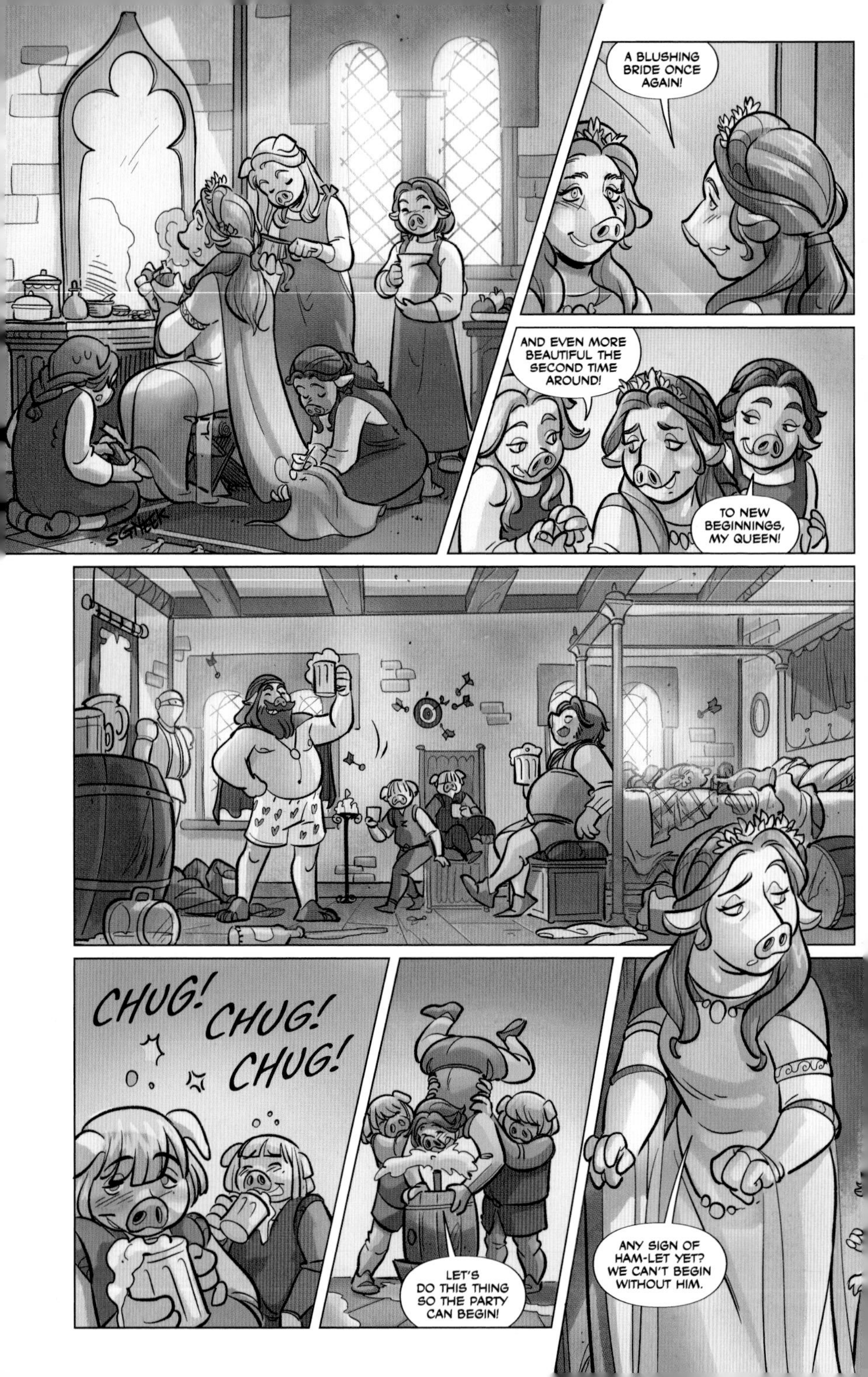

SGHEEK
A BLUSHING BRIDE ONCE AGAIN!
AND EVEN MORE BEAUTIFUL THE SECOND TIME AROUND!
TO NEW BEGINNINGS, MY QUEEN!
CHUG! CHUG! CHUG!
LET'S DO THIS THING SO THE PARTY CAN BEGIN!
ANY SIGN OF HAM-LET YET? WE CAN'T BEGIN WITHOUT HIM.

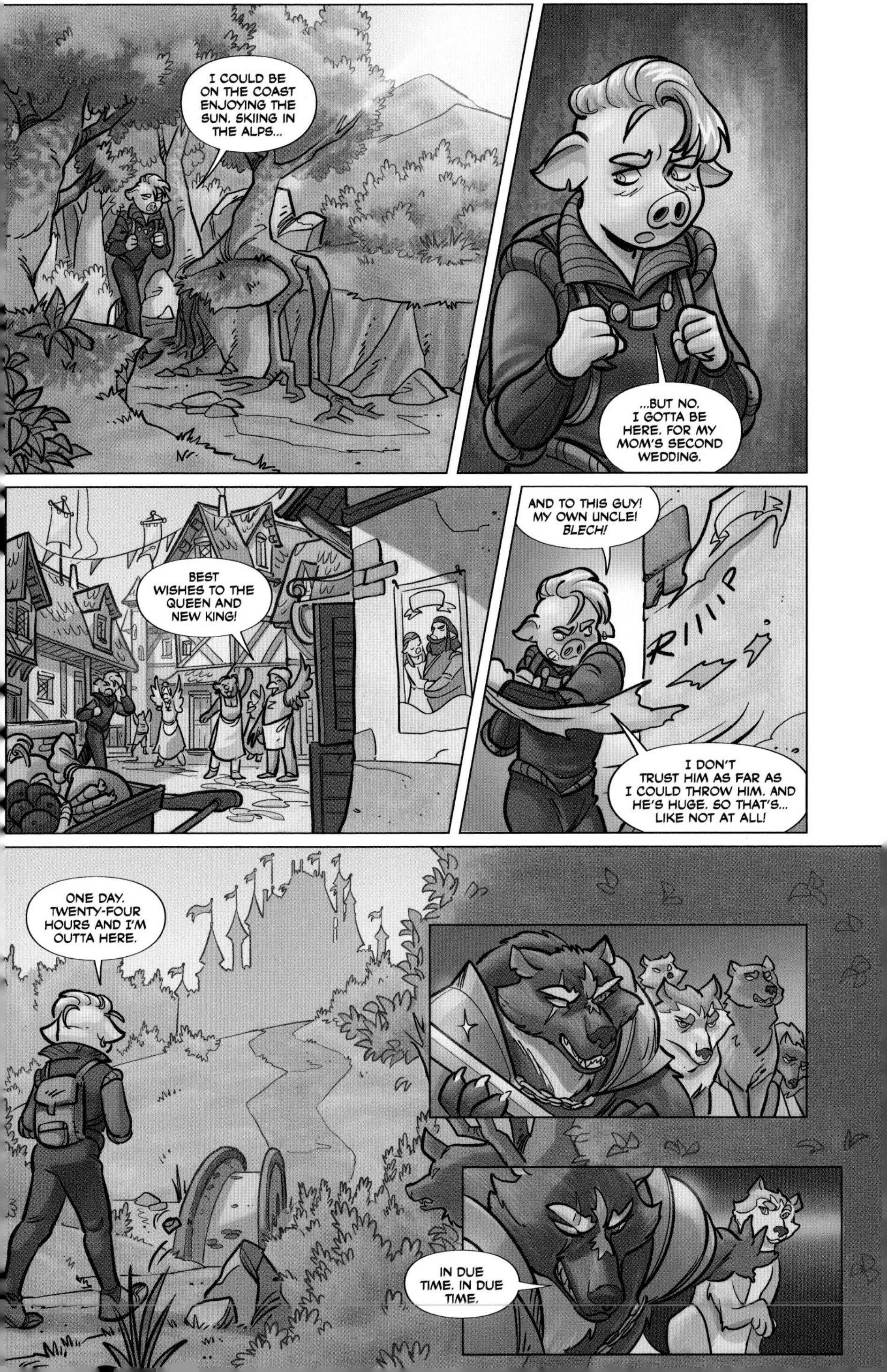
I COULD BE ON THE COAST ENJOYING THE SUN. SKIING IN THE ALPS...
...BUT NO. I GOTTA BE HERE. FOR MY MOM'S SECOND WEDDING.
BEST WISHES TO THE QUEEN AND NEW KING!
AND TO THIS GUY! MY OWN UNCLE! *BLECH!*
RIIIIP
I DON'T TRUST HIM AS FAR AS I COULD THROW HIM. AND HE'S HUGE. SO THAT'S... LIKE NOT AT ALL!
ONE DAY. TWENTY-FOUR HOURS AND I'M OUTTA HERE.
IN DUE TIME. IN DUE TIME.

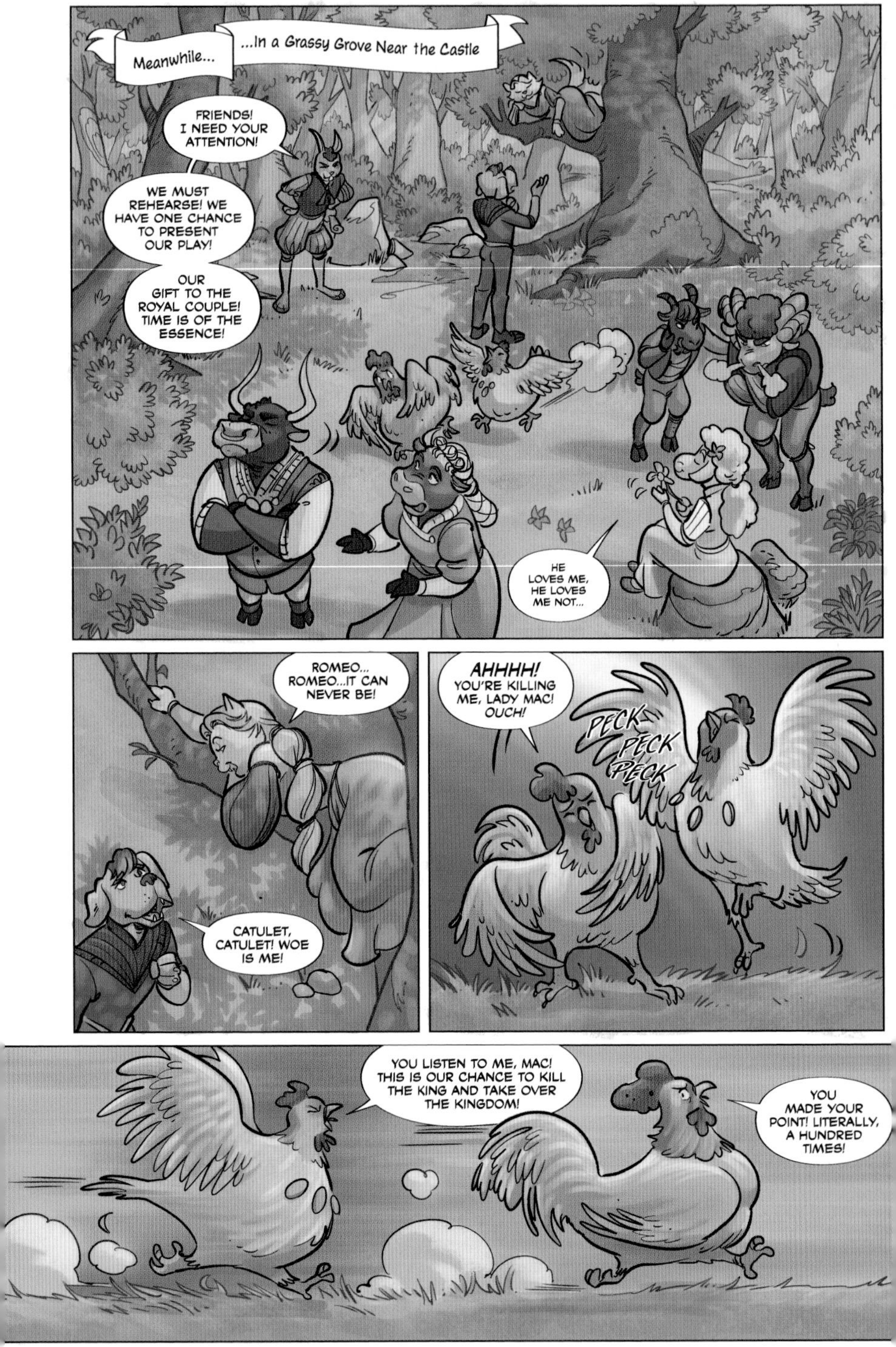
Meanwhile...
...In a Grassy Grove Near the Castle
FRIENDS! I NEED YOUR ATTENTION!
WE MUST REHEARSE! WE HAVE ONE CHANCE TO PRESENT OUR PLAY!
OUR GIFT TO THE ROYAL COUPLE! TIME IS OF THE ESSENCE!
HE LOVES ME, HE LOVES ME NOT...
ROMEO... ROMEO...IT CAN NEVER BE!
CATULET, CATULET! WOE IS ME!
AHHHH! YOU'RE KILLING ME, LADY MAC! OUCH!
PECK PECK PECK
YOU LISTEN TO ME, MAC! THIS IS OUR CHANCE TO KILL THE KING AND TAKE OVER THE KINGDOM!
YOU MADE YOUR POINT! LITERALLY, A HUNDRED TIMES!

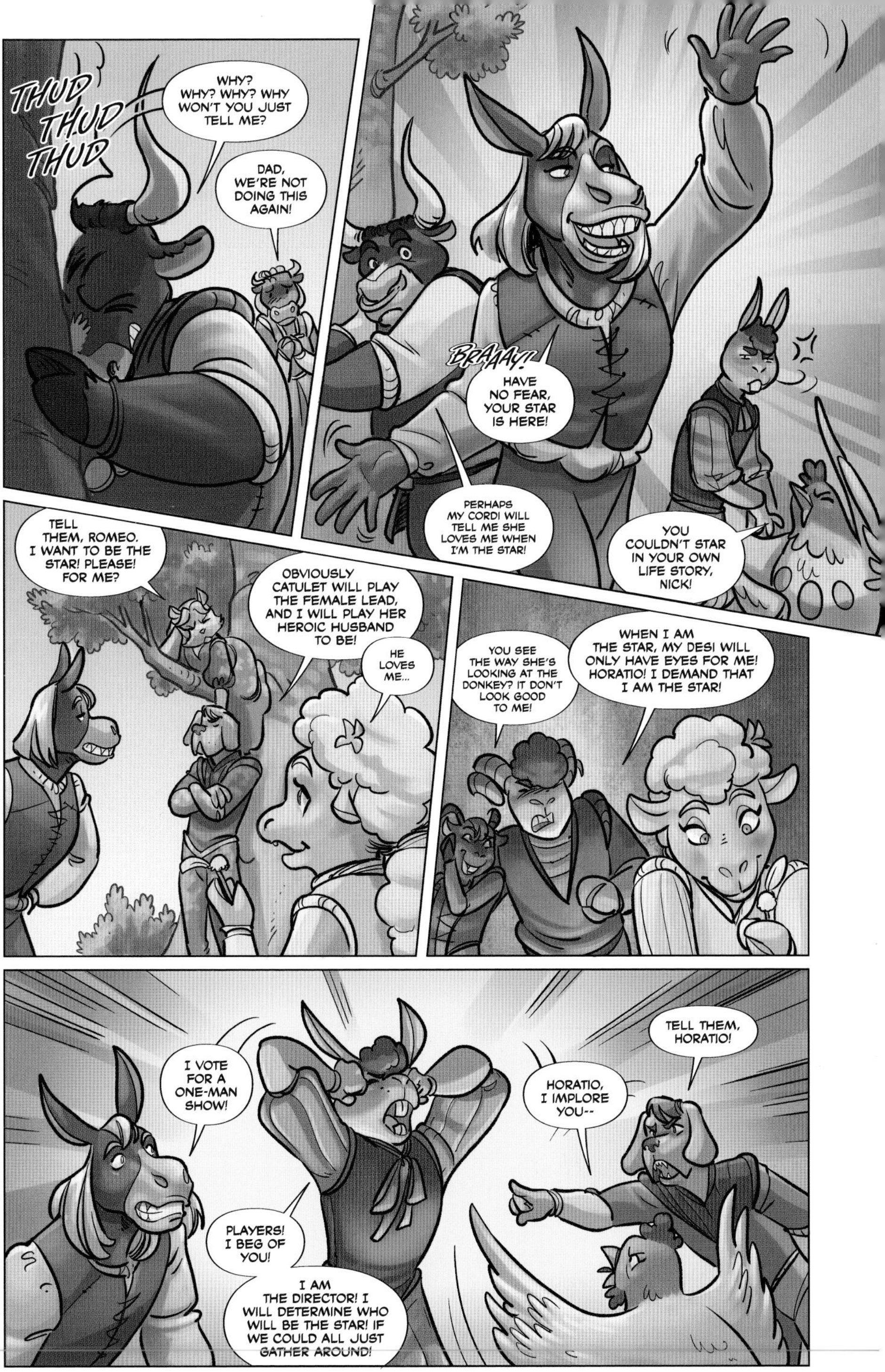
THUD THUD THUD
WHY? WHY? WHY? WHY WON'T YOU JUST TELL ME?
DAD, WE'RE NOT DOING THIS AGAIN!
BRAAAY!
HAVE NO FEAR, YOUR STAR IS HERE!
PERHAPS MY CORDI WILL TELL ME SHE LOVES ME WHEN I'M THE STAR!
YOU COULDN'T STAR IN YOUR OWN LIFE STORY, NICK!
TELL THEM, ROMEO. I WANT TO BE THE STAR! PLEASE! FOR ME?
OBVIOUSLY CATULET WILL PLAY THE FEMALE LEAD, AND I WILL PLAY HER HEROIC HUSBAND TO BE!
HE LOVES ME...
YOU SEE THE WAY SHE'S LOOKING AT THE DONKEY? IT DON'T LOOK GOOD TO ME!
WHEN I AM THE STAR, MY DESI WILL ONLY HAVE EYES FOR ME! HORATIO! I DEMAND THAT I AM THE STAR!
I VOTE FOR A ONE-MAN SHOW!
PLAYERS! I BEG OF YOU!
I AM THE DIRECTOR! I WILL DETERMINE WHO WILL BE THE STAR! IF WE COULD ALL JUST GATHER AROUND!
HORATIO, I IMPLORE YOU--
TELL THEM, HORATIO!

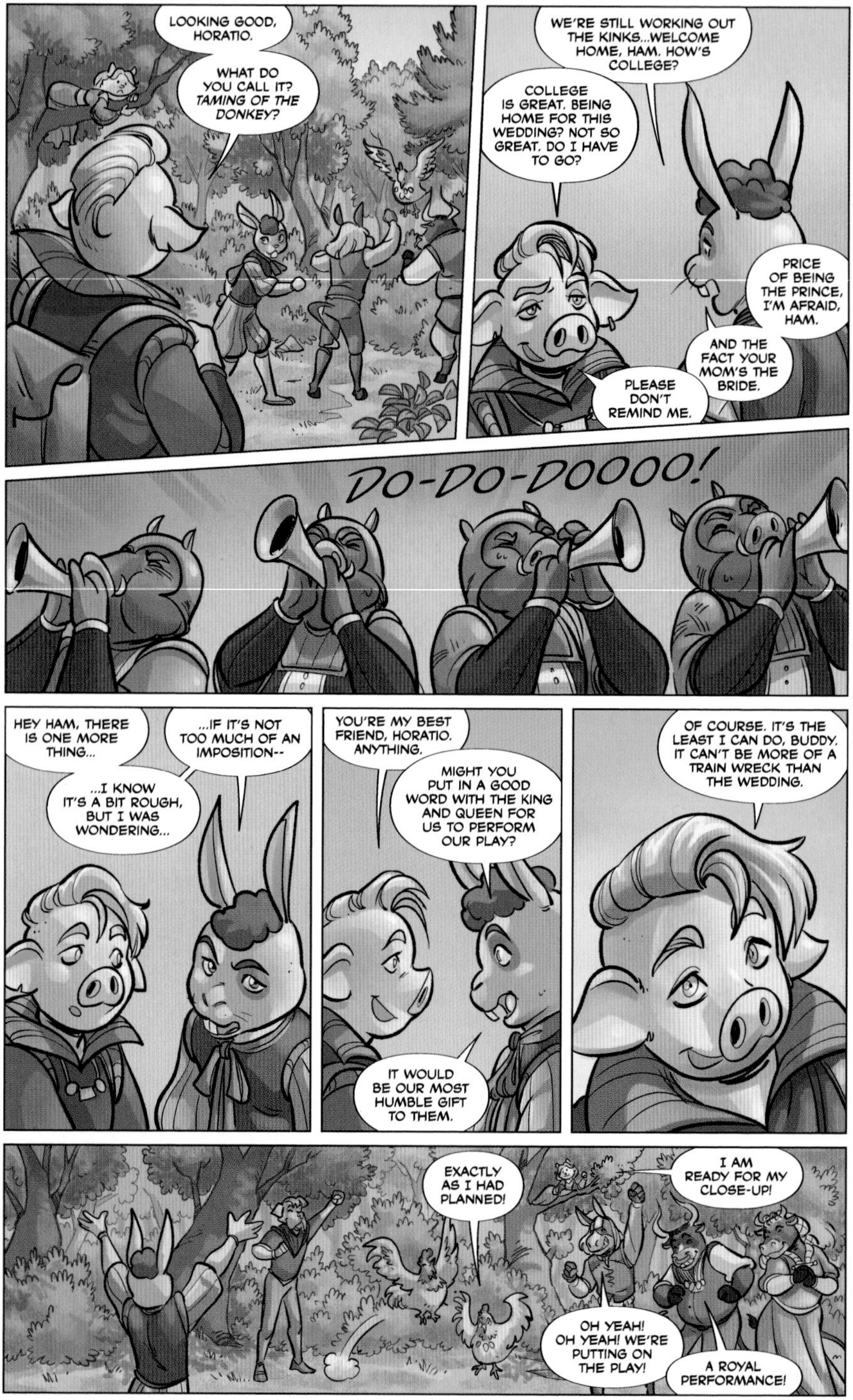
LOOKING GOOD, HORATIO.
WHAT DO YOU CALL IT? *TAMING OF THE DONKEY?*
WE'RE STILL WORKING OUT THE KINKS...WELCOME HOME, HAM. HOW'S COLLEGE?
COLLEGE IS GREAT. BEING HOME FOR THIS WEDDING? NOT SO GREAT. DO I HAVE TO GO?
PRICE OF BEING THE PRINCE, I'M AFRAID, HAM.
AND THE FACT YOUR MOM'S THE BRIDE.
PLEASE DON'T REMIND ME.
DO-DO-DOOOO!
HEY HAM, THERE IS ONE MORE THING...
...I KNOW IT'S A BIT ROUGH, BUT I WAS WONDERING...
...IF IT'S NOT TOO MUCH OF AN IMPOSITION--
YOU'RE MY BEST FRIEND, HORATIO. ANYTHING.
MIGHT YOU PUT IN A GOOD WORD WITH THE KING AND QUEEN FOR US TO PERFORM OUR PLAY?
IT WOULD BE OUR MOST HUMBLE GIFT TO THEM.
OF COURSE. IT'S THE LEAST I CAN DO, BUDDY. IT CAN'T BE MORE OF A TRAIN WRECK THAN THE WEDDING.
EXACTLY AS I HAD PLANNED!
I AM READY FOR MY CLOSE-UP!
OH YEAH! OH YEAH! WE'RE PUTTING ON THE PLAY!
A ROYAL PERFORMANCE!

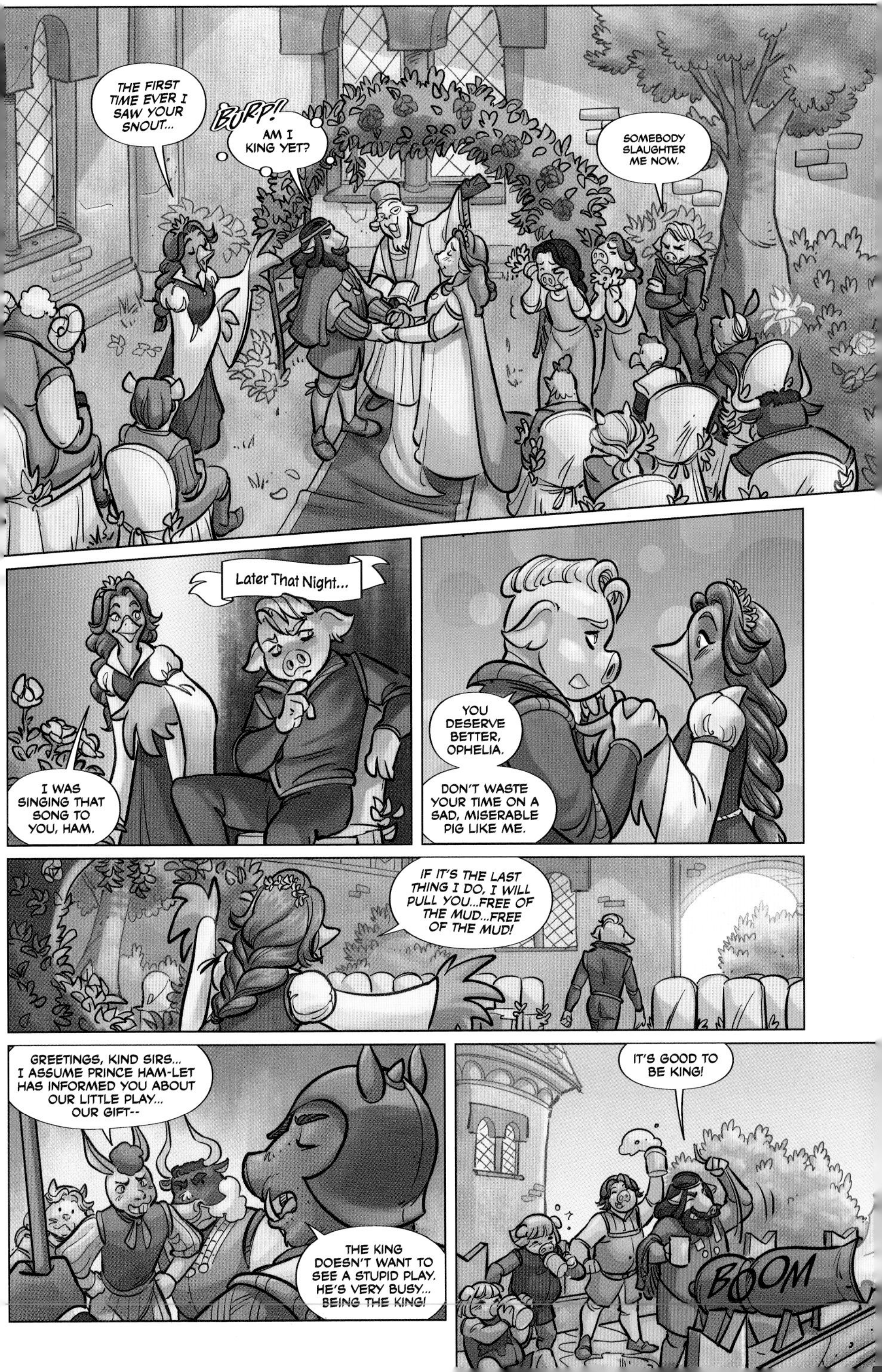
THE FIRST TIME EVER I SAW YOUR SNOUT...
BURP!
AM I KING YET?
SOMEBODY SLAUGHTER ME NOW.
Later That Night...
I WAS SINGING THAT SONG TO YOU, HAM.
YOU DESERVE BETTER, OPHELIA.
DON'T WASTE YOUR TIME ON A SAD, MISERABLE PIG LIKE ME.
IF IT'S THE LAST THING I DO, I WILL PULL YOU...FREE OF THE MUD...FREE OF THE MUD!
GREETINGS, KIND SIRS... I ASSUME PRINCE HAM-LET HAS INFORMED YOU ABOUT OUR LITTLE PLAY... OUR GIFT--
THE KING DOESN'T WANT TO SEE A STUPID PLAY. HE'S VERY BUSY... BEING THE KING!
IT'S GOOD TO BE KING!
BOOM

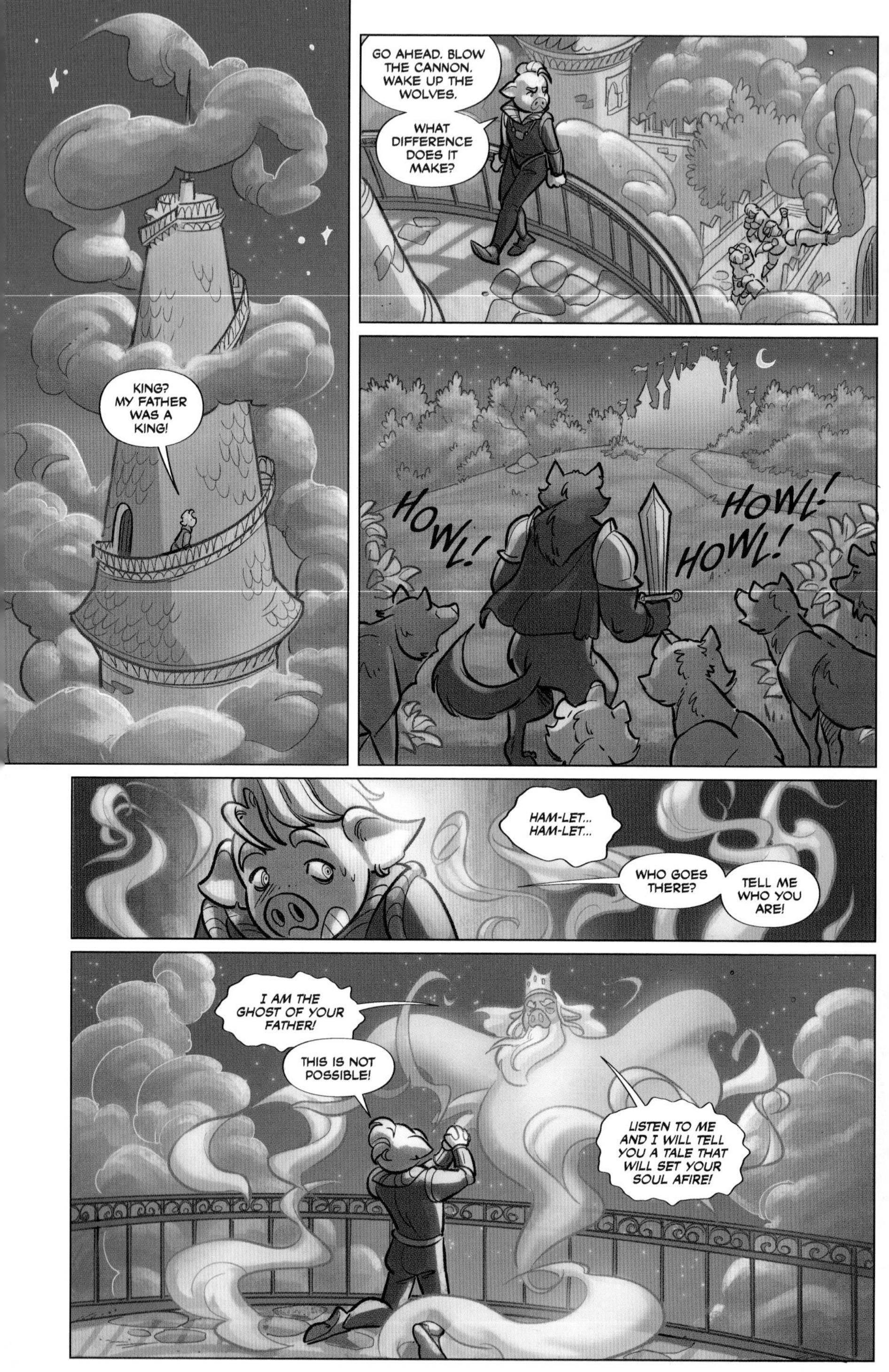
KING? MY FATHER WAS A KING!
GO AHEAD. BLOW THE CANNON. WAKE UP THE WOLVES.
WHAT DIFFERENCE DOES IT MAKE?
HOWL!
HOWL!
HOWL!
HAM-LET... HAM-LET...
WHO GOES THERE?
TELL ME WHO YOU ARE!
I AM THE GHOST OF YOUR FATHER!
THIS IS NOT POSSIBLE!
LISTEN TO ME AND I WILL TELL YOU A TALE THAT WILL SET YOUR SOUL AFIRE!

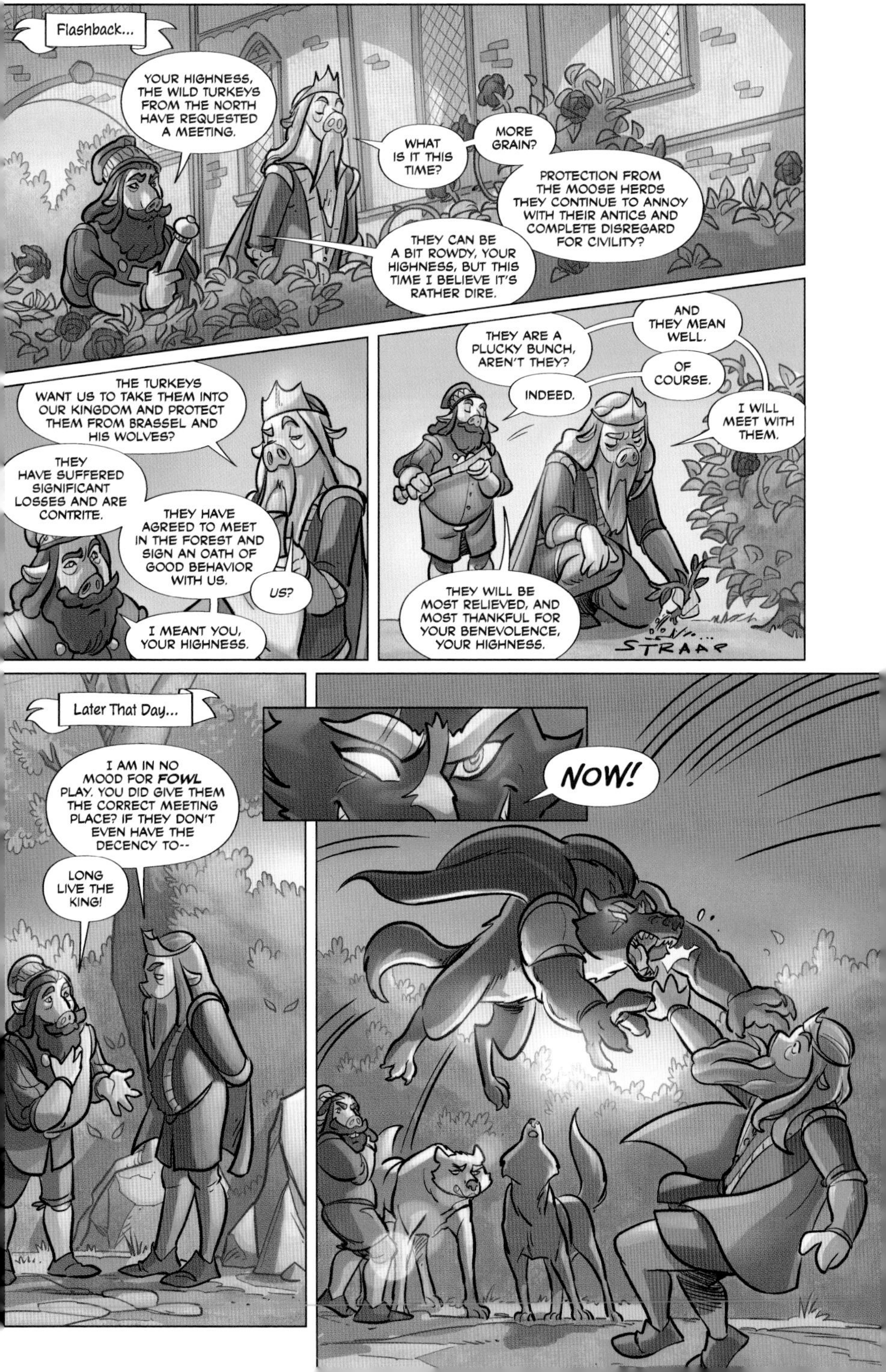
Flashback...
YOUR HIGHNESS, THE WILD TURKEYS FROM THE NORTH HAVE REQUESTED A MEETING.
WHAT IS IT THIS TIME?
MORE GRAIN?
PROTECTION FROM THE MOOSE HERDS THEY CONTINUE TO ANNOY WITH THEIR ANTICS AND COMPLETE DISREGARD FOR CIVILITY?
THEY CAN BE A BIT ROWDY, YOUR HIGHNESS, BUT THIS TIME I BELIEVE IT'S RATHER DIRE.
THE TURKEYS WANT US TO TAKE THEM INTO OUR KINGDOM AND PROTECT THEM FROM BRASSEL AND HIS WOLVES?
THEY HAVE SUFFERED SIGNIFICANT LOSSES AND ARE CONTRITE.
THEY HAVE AGREED TO MEET IN THE FOREST AND SIGN AN OATH OF GOOD BEHAVIOR WITH US.
US?
I MEANT YOU, YOUR HIGHNESS.
THEY ARE A PLUCKY BUNCH, AREN'T THEY?
AND THEY MEAN WELL.
INDEED.
OF COURSE.
I WILL MEET WITH THEM.
THEY WILL BE MOST RELIEVED, AND MOST THANKFUL FOR YOUR BENEVOLENCE, YOUR HIGHNESS.
STRAAP
Later That Day...
I AM IN NO MOOD FOR **FOWL** PLAY. YOU DID GIVE THEM THE CORRECT MEETING PLACE? IF THEY DON'T EVEN HAVE THE DECENCY TO--
LONG LIVE THE KING!
NOW!

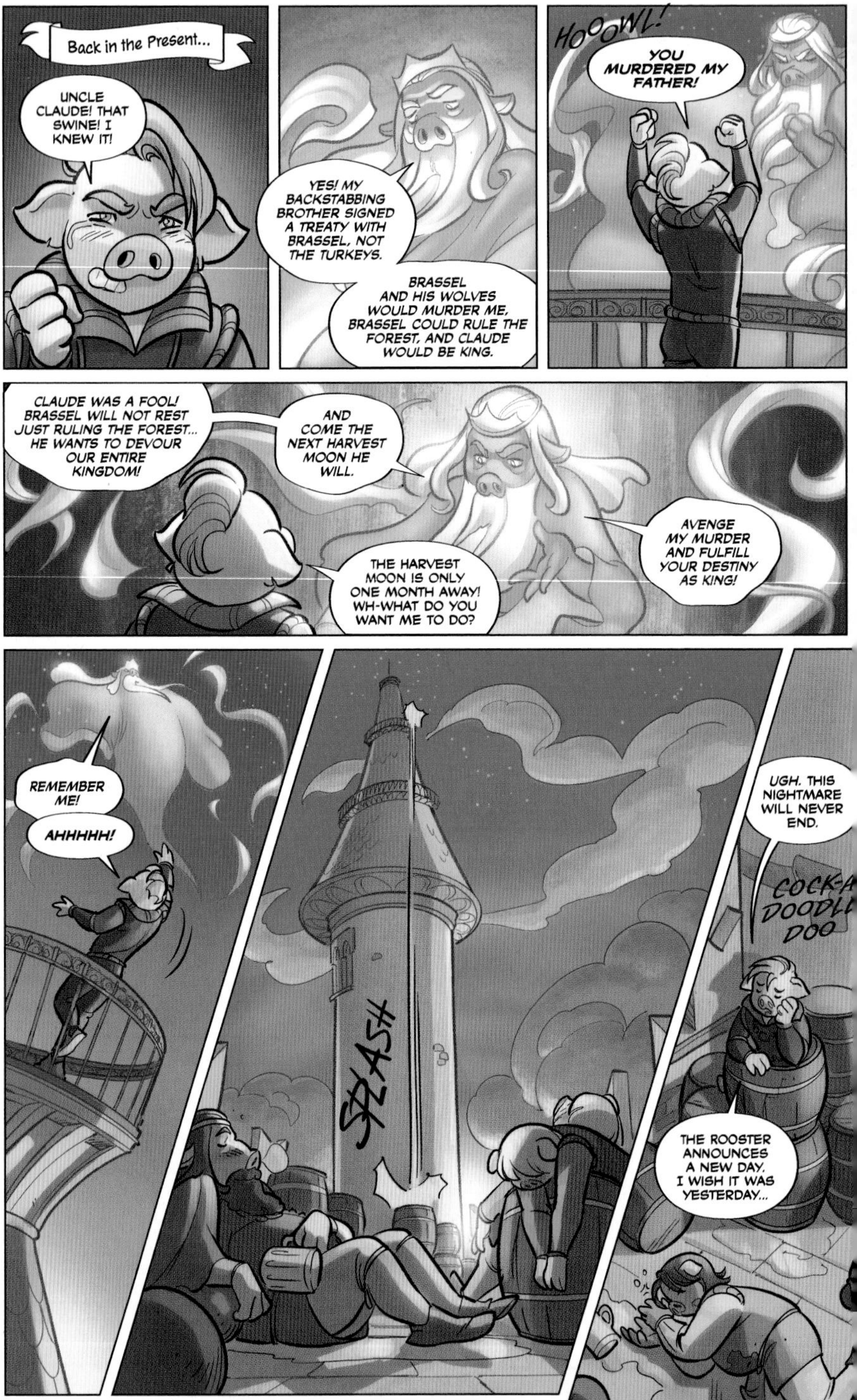
Back in the Present...
UNCLE CLAUDE! THAT SWINE! I KNEW IT!
YES! MY BACKSTABBING BROTHER SIGNED A TREATY WITH BRASSEL, NOT THE TURKEYS.
BRASSEL AND HIS WOLVES WOULD MURDER ME, BRASSEL COULD RULE THE FOREST, AND CLAUDE WOULD BE KING.
HOOOOWL!
YOU MURDERED MY FATHER!
CLAUDE WAS A FOOL! BRASSEL WILL NOT REST JUST RULING THE FOREST... HE WANTS TO DEVOUR OUR ENTIRE KINGDOM!
AND COME THE NEXT HARVEST MOON HE WILL.
THE HARVEST MOON IS ONLY ONE MONTH AWAY! WH-WHAT DO YOU WANT ME TO DO?
AVENGE MY MURDER AND FULFILL YOUR DESTINY AS KING!
REMEMBER ME!
AHHHHH!
SPLASH
UGH. THIS NIGHTMARE WILL NEVER END.
THE ROOSTER ANNOUNCES A NEW DAY. I WISH IT WAS YESTERDAY...

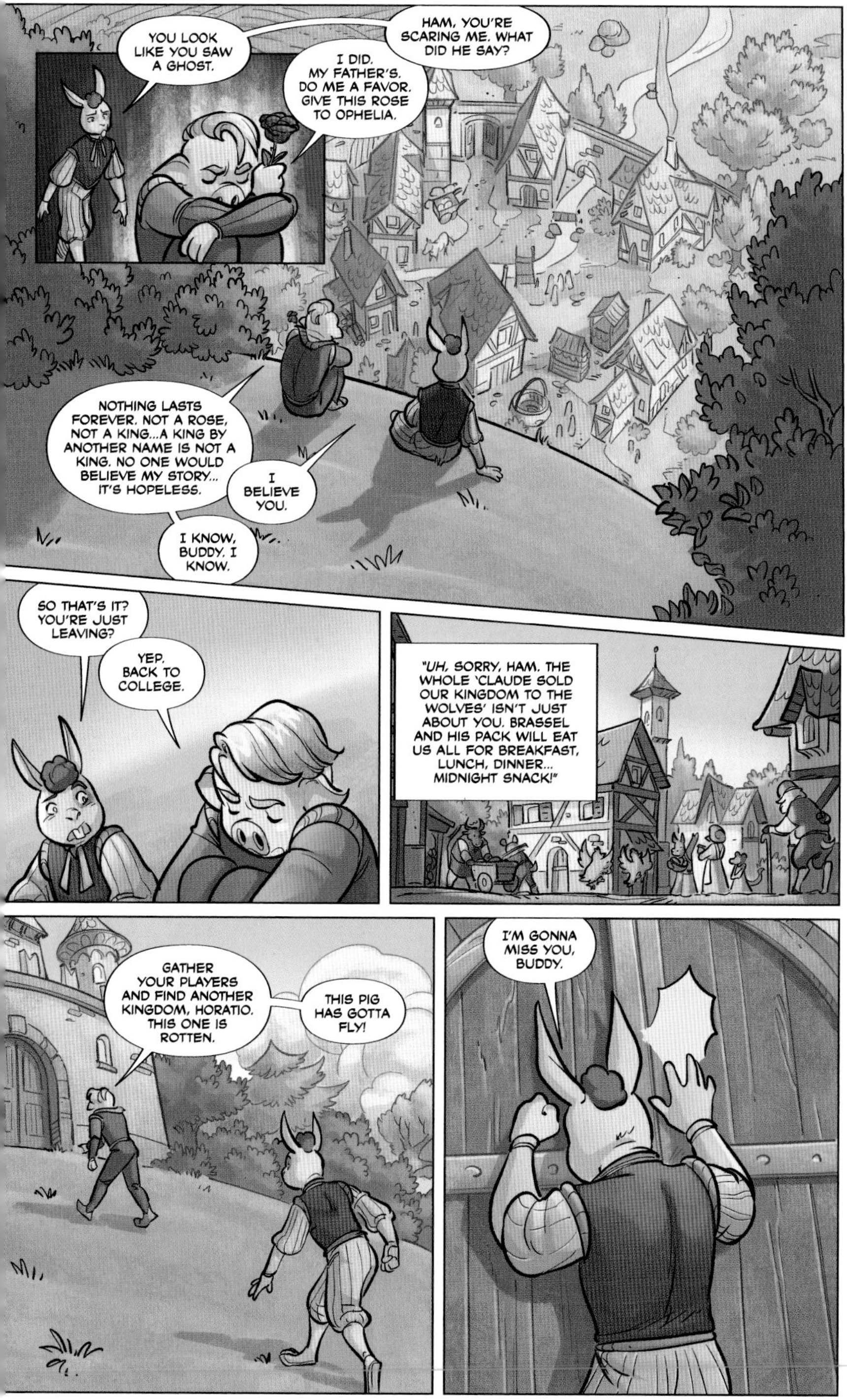
YOU LOOK LIKE YOU SAW A GHOST.
I DID. MY FATHER'S. DO ME A FAVOR. GIVE THIS ROSE TO OPHELIA.
HAM, YOU'RE SCARING ME. WHAT DID HE SAY?
NOTHING LASTS FOREVER. NOT A ROSE, NOT A KING...A KING BY ANOTHER NAME IS NOT A KING. NO ONE WOULD BELIEVE MY STORY... IT'S HOPELESS.
I BELIEVE YOU.
I KNOW, BUDDY. I KNOW.
SO THAT'S IT? YOU'RE JUST LEAVING?
YEP. BACK TO COLLEGE.
"UH, SORRY, HAM. THE WHOLE 'CLAUDE SOLD OUR KINGDOM TO THE WOLVES' ISN'T JUST ABOUT YOU. BRASSEL AND HIS PACK WILL EAT US ALL FOR BREAKFAST, LUNCH, DINNER... MIDNIGHT SNACK!"
GATHER YOUR PLAYERS AND FIND ANOTHER KINGDOM, HORATIO. THIS ONE IS ROTTEN.
THIS PIG HAS GOTTA FLY!
I'M GONNA MISS YOU, BUDDY.

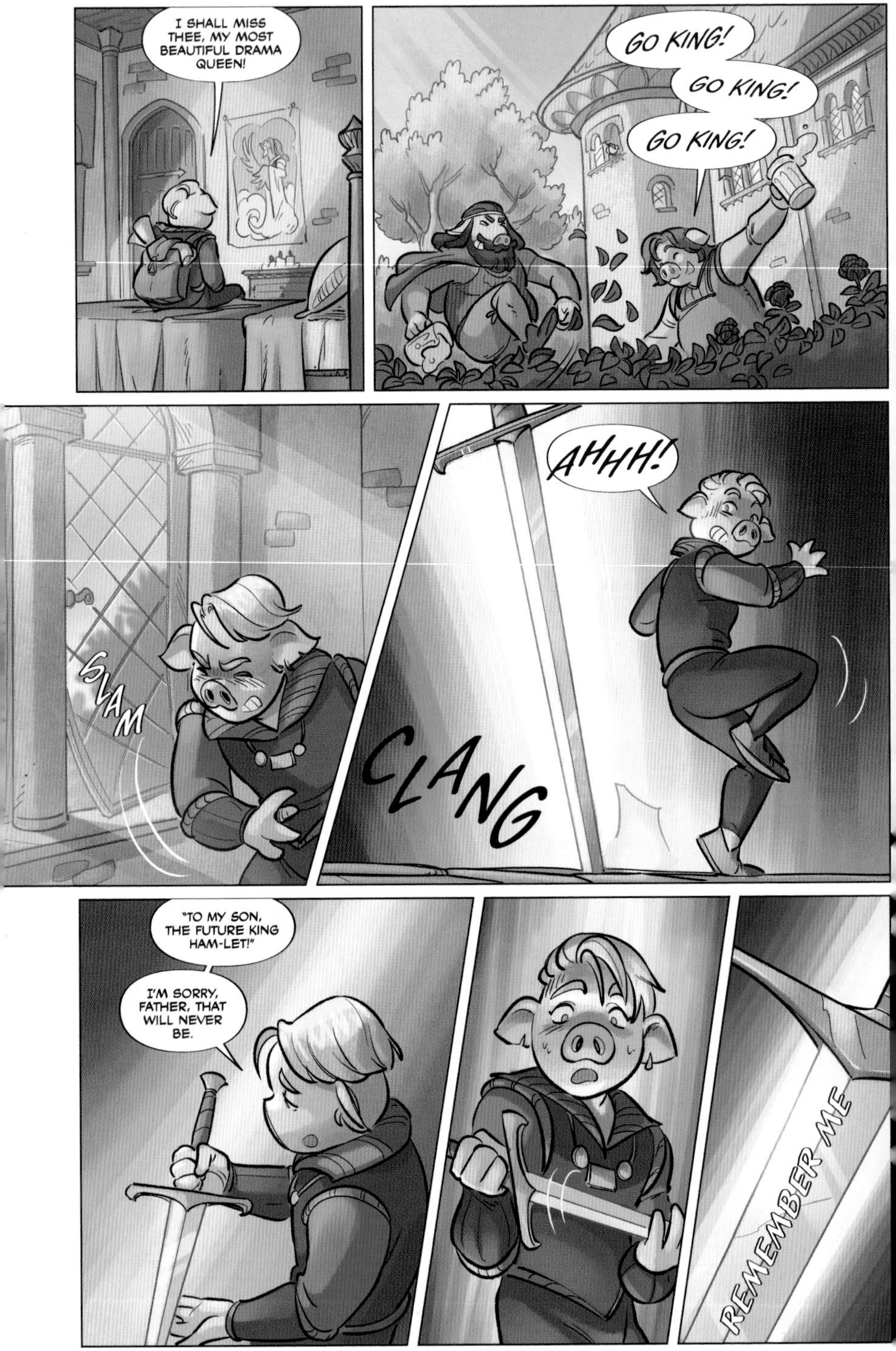
I SHALL MISS THEE, MY MOST BEAUTIFUL DRAMA QUEEN!
GO KING!
GO KING!
GO KING!
SLAM
AHHH!
CLANG
"TO MY SON, THE FUTURE KING HAM-LET!"
I'M SORRY, FATHER, THAT WILL NEVER BE.
REMEMBER ME

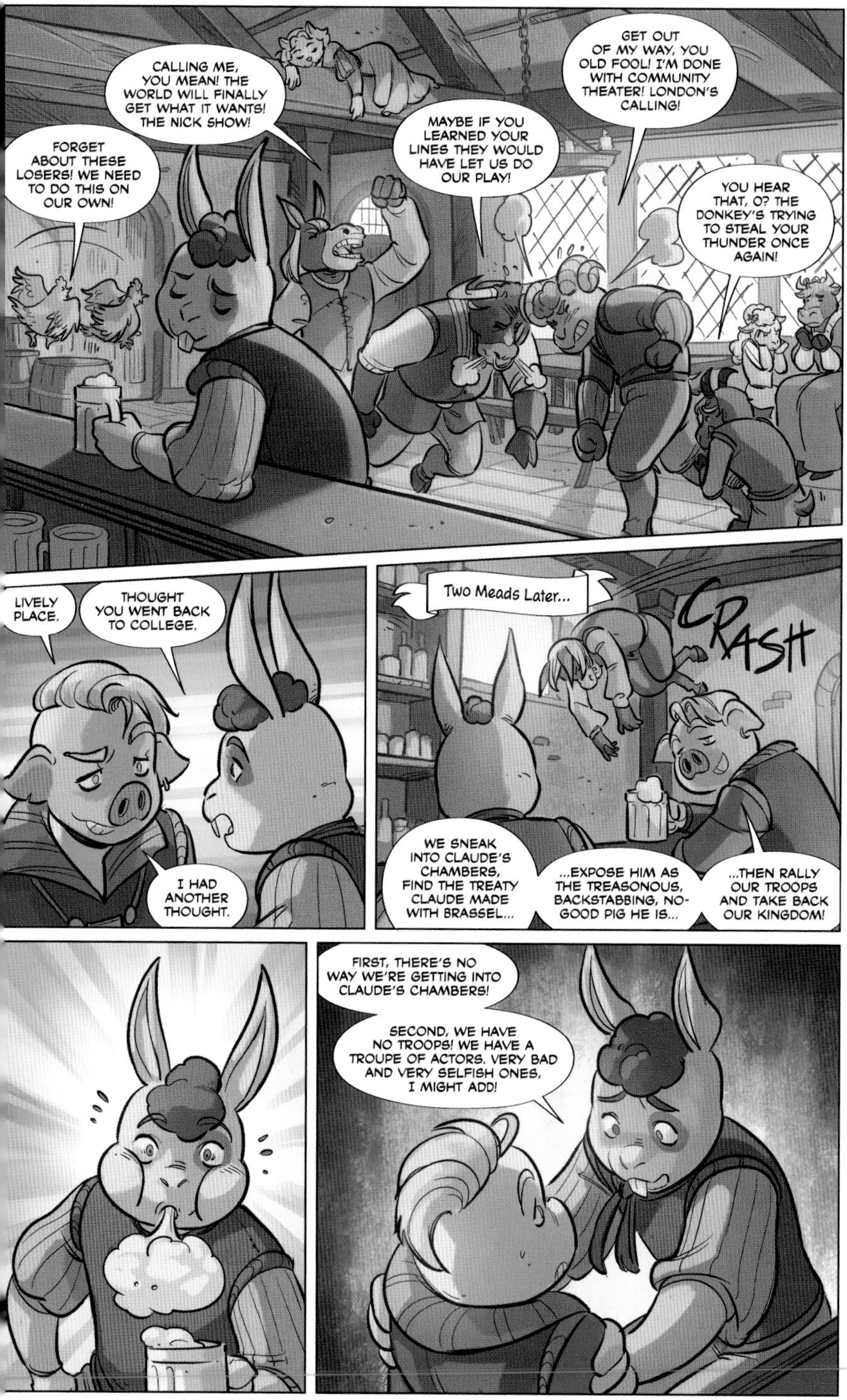
FORGET ABOUT THESE LOSERS! WE NEED TO DO THIS ON OUR OWN!
CALLING ME, YOU MEAN! THE WORLD WILL FINALLY GET WHAT IT WANTS! THE NICK SHOW!
MAYBE IF YOU LEARNED YOUR LINES THEY WOULD HAVE LET US DO OUR PLAY!
GET OUT OF MY WAY, YOU OLD FOOL! I'M DONE WITH COMMUNITY THEATER! LONDON'S CALLING!
YOU HEAR THAT, O? THE DONKEY'S TRYING TO STEAL YOUR THUNDER ONCE AGAIN!
LIVELY PLACE.
THOUGHT YOU WENT BACK TO COLLEGE.
I HAD ANOTHER THOUGHT.
Two Meads Later...
CRASH
WE SNEAK INTO CLAUDE'S CHAMBERS, FIND THE TREATY CLAUDE MADE WITH BRASSEL...
...EXPOSE HIM AS THE TREASONOUS, BACKSTABBING, NO-GOOD PIG HE IS...
...THEN RALLY OUR TROOPS AND TAKE BACK OUR KINGDOM!
FIRST, THERE'S NO WAY WE'RE GETTING INTO CLAUDE'S CHAMBERS!
SECOND, WE HAVE NO TROOPS! WE HAVE A TROUPE OF ACTORS. VERY BAD AND VERY SELFISH ONES, I MIGHT ADD!

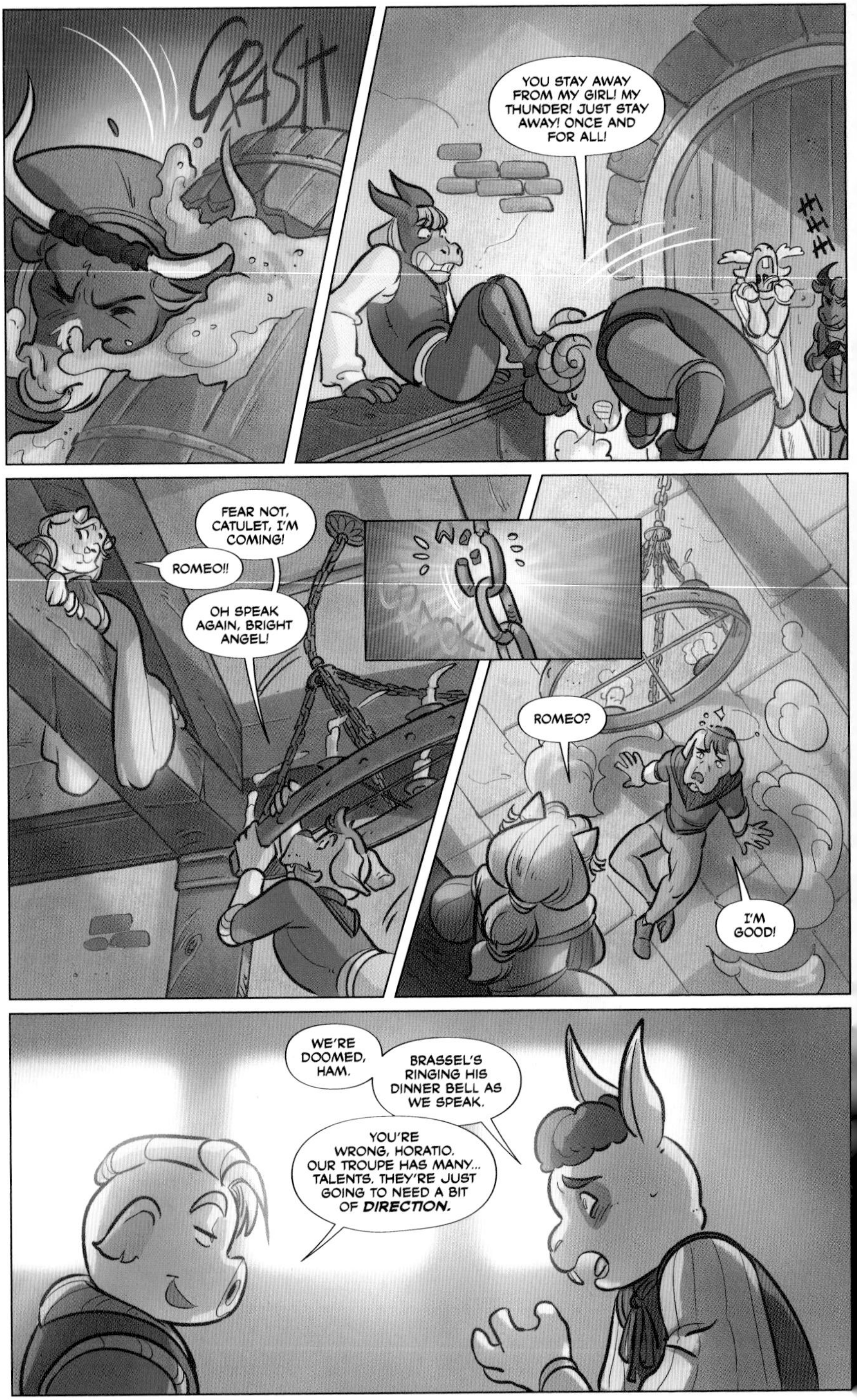
CRASH
YOU STAY AWAY FROM MY GIRL! MY THUNDER! JUST STAY AWAY! ONCE AND FOR ALL!
FEAR NOT, CATULET, I'M COMING!
ROMEO!!
OH SPEAK AGAIN, BRIGHT ANGEL!
CRACK
ROMEO?
I'M GOOD!
WE'RE DOOMED, HAM.
BRASSEL'S RINGING HIS DINNER BELL AS WE SPEAK.
YOU'RE WRONG, HORATIO. OUR TROUPE HAS MANY... TALENTS. THEY'RE JUST GOING TO NEED A BIT OF ***DIRECTION.***

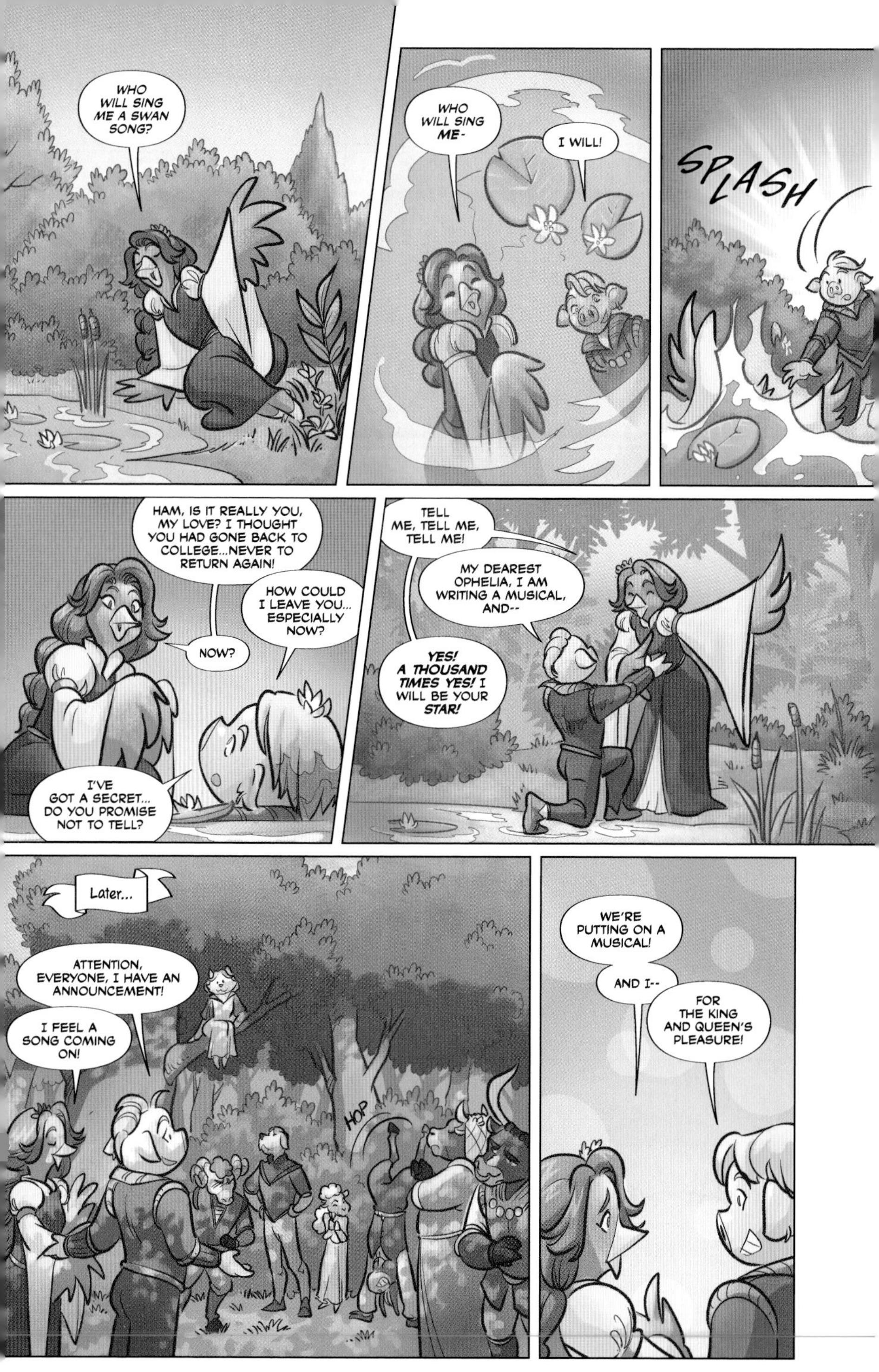
WHO WILL SING ME A SWAN SONG?
WHO WILL SING ME-
I WILL!
SPLASH
HAM, IS IT REALLY YOU, MY LOVE? I THOUGHT YOU HAD GONE BACK TO COLLEGE...NEVER TO RETURN AGAIN!
HOW COULD I LEAVE YOU... ESPECIALLY NOW?
NOW?
I'VE GOT A SECRET... DO YOU PROMISE NOT TO TELL?
TELL ME, TELL ME, TELL ME!
MY DEAREST OPHELIA, I AM WRITING A MUSICAL, AND--
YES! A THOUSAND TIMES YES! I WILL BE YOUR STAR!
Later...
ATTENTION, EVERYONE, I HAVE AN ANNOUNCEMENT!
I FEEL A SONG COMING ON!
HOP
WE'RE PUTTING ON A MUSICAL!
AND I--
FOR THE KING AND QUEEN'S PLEASURE!

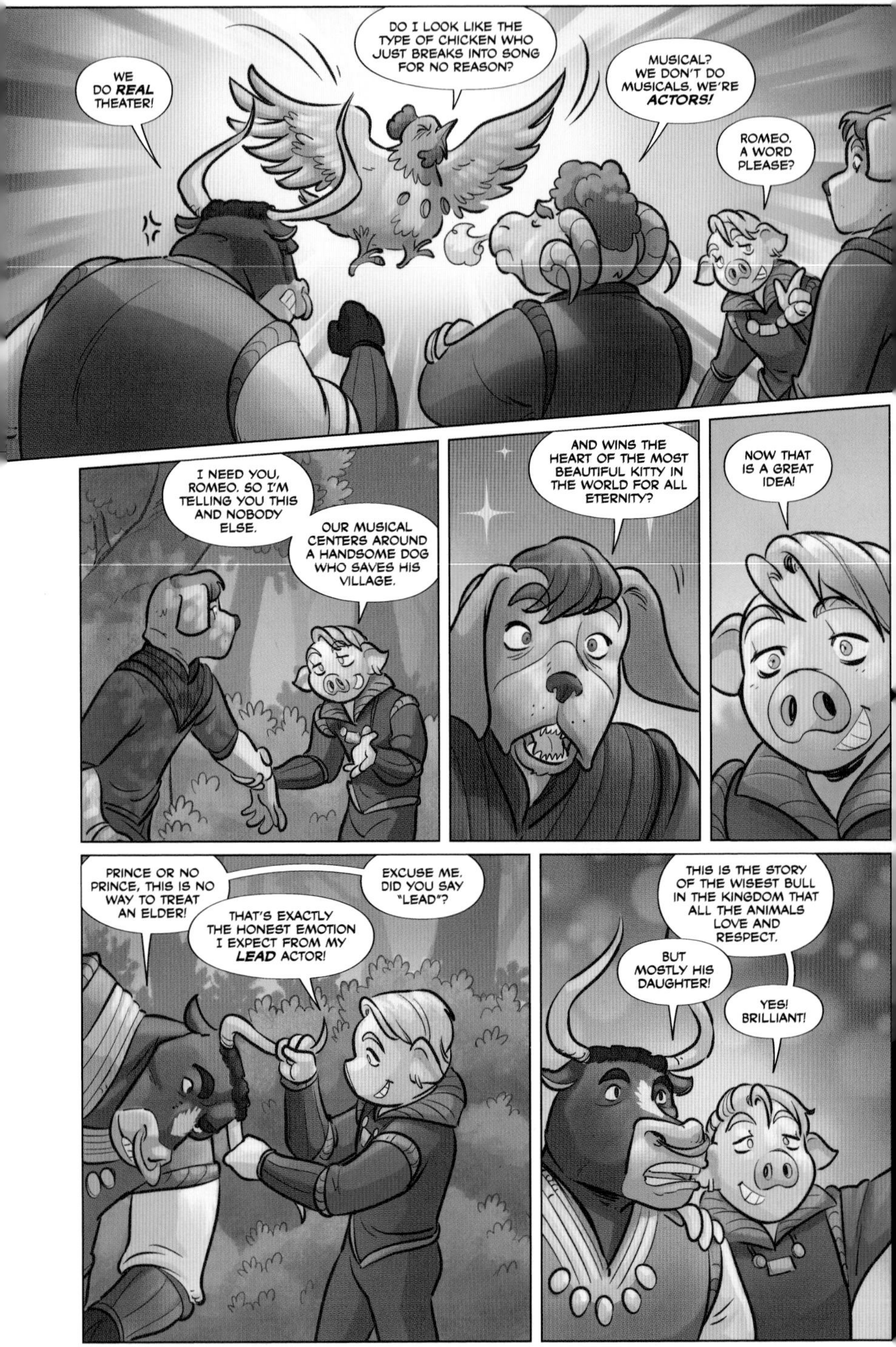
WE DO REAL THEATER!
DO I LOOK LIKE THE TYPE OF CHICKEN WHO JUST BREAKS INTO SONG FOR NO REASON?
MUSICAL? WE DON'T DO MUSICALS. WE'RE ACTORS!
ROMEO, A WORD PLEASE?
I NEED YOU, ROMEO, SO I'M TELLING YOU THIS AND NOBODY ELSE.
OUR MUSICAL CENTERS AROUND A HANDSOME DOG WHO SAVES HIS VILLAGE.
AND WINS THE HEART OF THE MOST BEAUTIFUL KITTY IN THE WORLD FOR ALL ETERNITY?
NOW THAT IS A GREAT IDEA!
PRINCE OR NO PRINCE, THIS IS NO WAY TO TREAT AN ELDER!
THAT'S EXACTLY THE HONEST EMOTION I EXPECT FROM MY LEAD ACTOR!
EXCUSE ME. DID YOU SAY "LEAD"?
THIS IS THE STORY OF THE WISEST BULL IN THE KINGDOM THAT ALL THE ANIMALS LOVE AND RESPECT.
BUT MOSTLY HIS DAUGHTER!
YES! BRILLIANT!

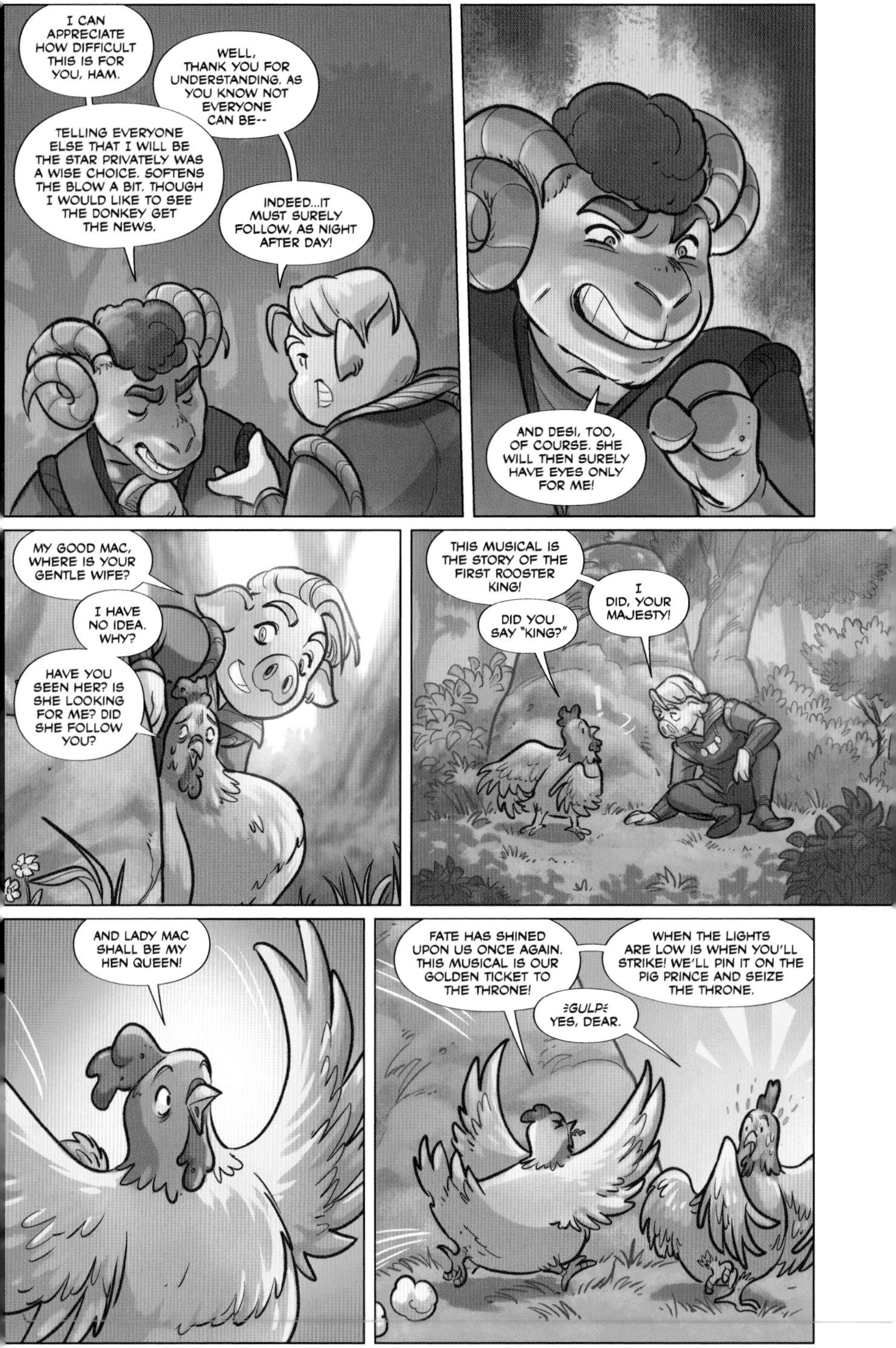
I CAN APPRECIATE HOW DIFFICULT THIS IS FOR YOU, HAM.
WELL, THANK YOU FOR UNDERSTANDING. AS YOU KNOW NOT EVERYONE CAN BE--
TELLING EVERYONE ELSE THAT I WILL BE THE STAR PRIVATELY WAS A WISE CHOICE. SOFTENS THE BLOW A BIT. THOUGH I WOULD LIKE TO SEE THE DONKEY GET THE NEWS.
INDEED...IT MUST SURELY FOLLOW, AS NIGHT AFTER DAY!
AND DESI, TOO, OF COURSE. SHE WILL THEN SURELY HAVE EYES ONLY FOR ME!
MY GOOD MAC, WHERE IS YOUR GENTLE WIFE?
I HAVE NO IDEA. WHY?
HAVE YOU SEEN HER? IS SHE LOOKING FOR ME? DID SHE FOLLOW YOU?
THIS MUSICAL IS THE STORY OF THE FIRST ROOSTER KING!
DID YOU SAY "KING?"
I DID, YOUR MAJESTY!
AND LADY MAC SHALL BE MY HEN QUEEN!
FATE HAS SHINED UPON US ONCE AGAIN. THIS MUSICAL IS OUR GOLDEN TICKET TO THE THRONE!
WHEN THE LIGHTS ARE LOW IS WHEN YOU'LL STRIKE! WE'LL PIN IT ON THE PIG PRINCE AND SEIZE THE THRONE.
GULP
YES, DEAR.

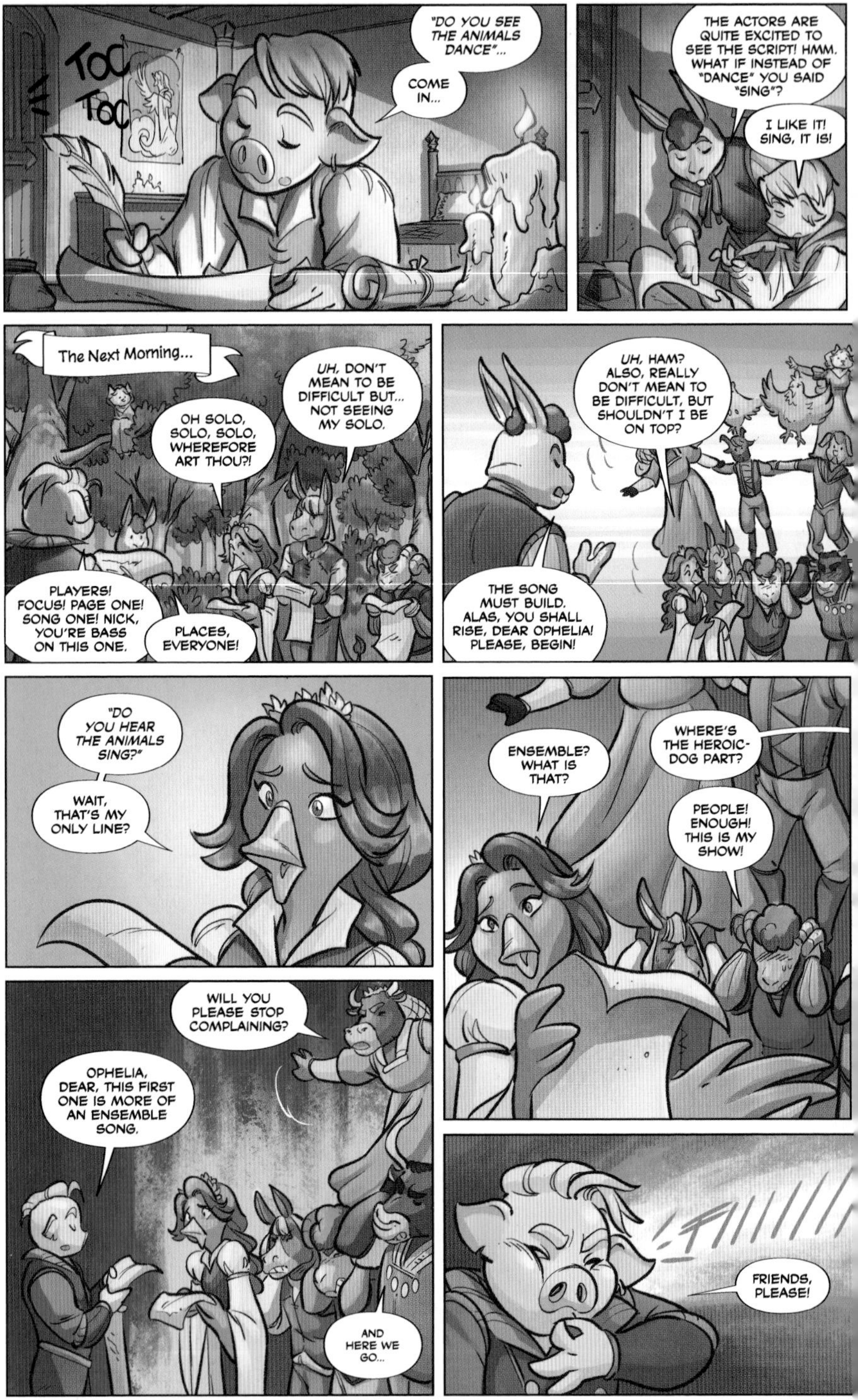
TOC TOC
"DO YOU SEE THE ANIMALS DANCE"...
COME IN...
THE ACTORS ARE QUITE EXCITED TO SEE THE SCRIPT! HMM. WHAT IF INSTEAD OF "DANCE" YOU SAID "SING"?
I LIKE IT! SING, IT IS!
The Next Morning...
UH, DON'T MEAN TO BE DIFFICULT BUT... NOT SEEING MY SOLO.
OH SOLO, SOLO, SOLO, WHEREFORE ART THOU?!
PLAYERS! FOCUS! PAGE ONE! SONG ONE! NICK, YOU'RE BASS ON THIS ONE.
PLACES, EVERYONE!
UH, HAM? ALSO, REALLY DON'T MEAN TO BE DIFFICULT, BUT SHOULDN'T I BE ON TOP?
THE SONG MUST BUILD. ALAS, YOU SHALL RISE, DEAR OPHELIA! PLEASE, BEGIN!
"DO YOU HEAR THE ANIMALS SING?"
WAIT, THAT'S MY ONLY LINE?
WILL YOU PLEASE STOP COMPLAINING?
OPHELIA, DEAR, THIS FIRST ONE IS MORE OF AN ENSEMBLE SONG.
AND HERE WE GO...
ENSEMBLE? WHAT IS THAT?
WHERE'S THE HEROIC-DOG PART?
PEOPLE! ENOUGH! THIS IS MY SHOW!
FRIENDS, PLEASE!

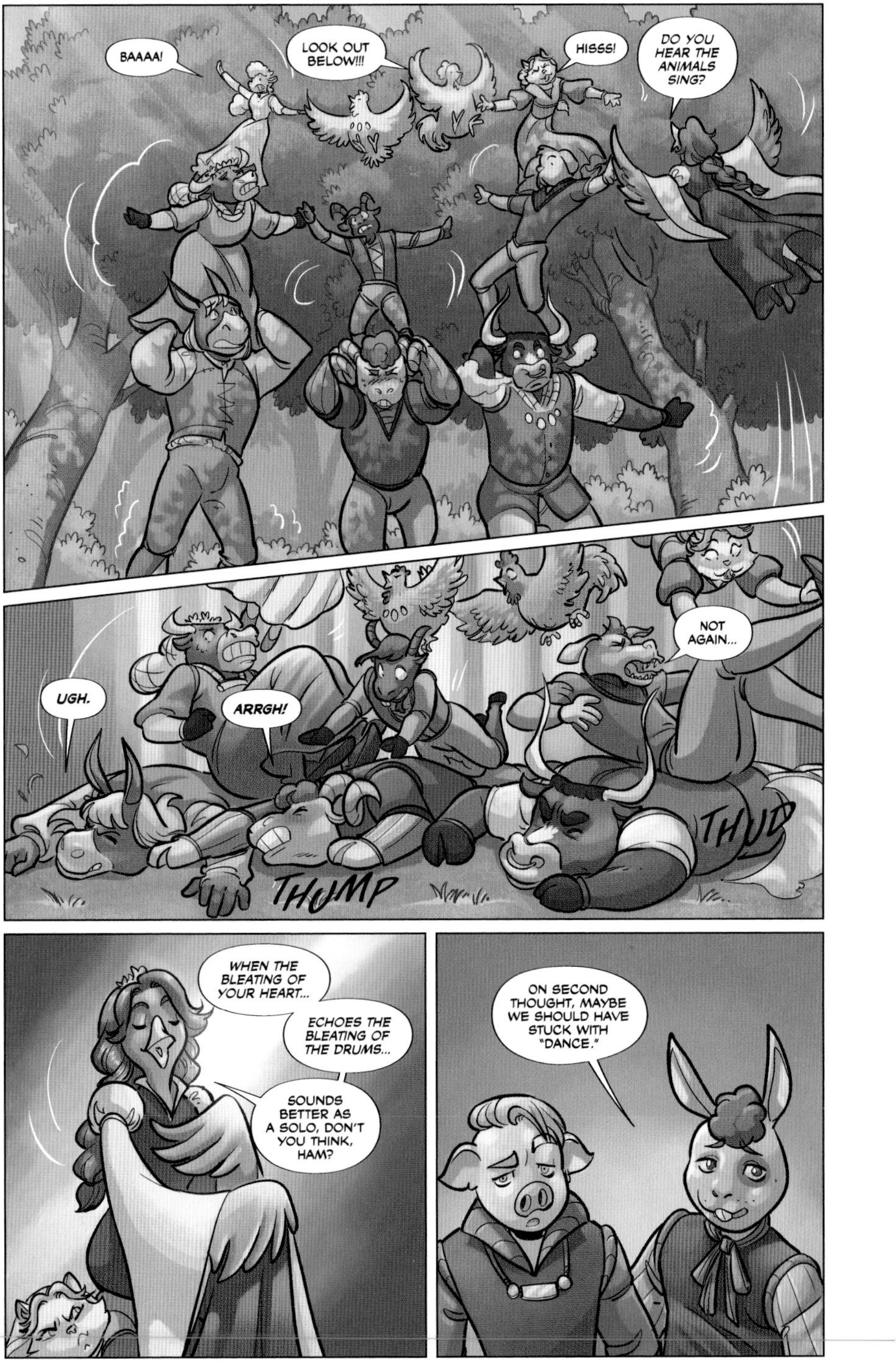

BAAAA!
LOOK OUT BELOW!!!
HISSS!
DO YOU HEAR THE ANIMALS SING?
UGH.
ARRGH!
NOT AGAIN...
THUMP
THUD
WHEN THE BLEATING OF YOUR HEART...
ECHOES THE BLEATING OF THE DRUMS...
SOUNDS BETTER AS A SOLO, DON'T YOU THINK, HAM?
ON SECOND THOUGHT, MAYBE WE SHOULD HAVE STUCK WITH "DANCE."

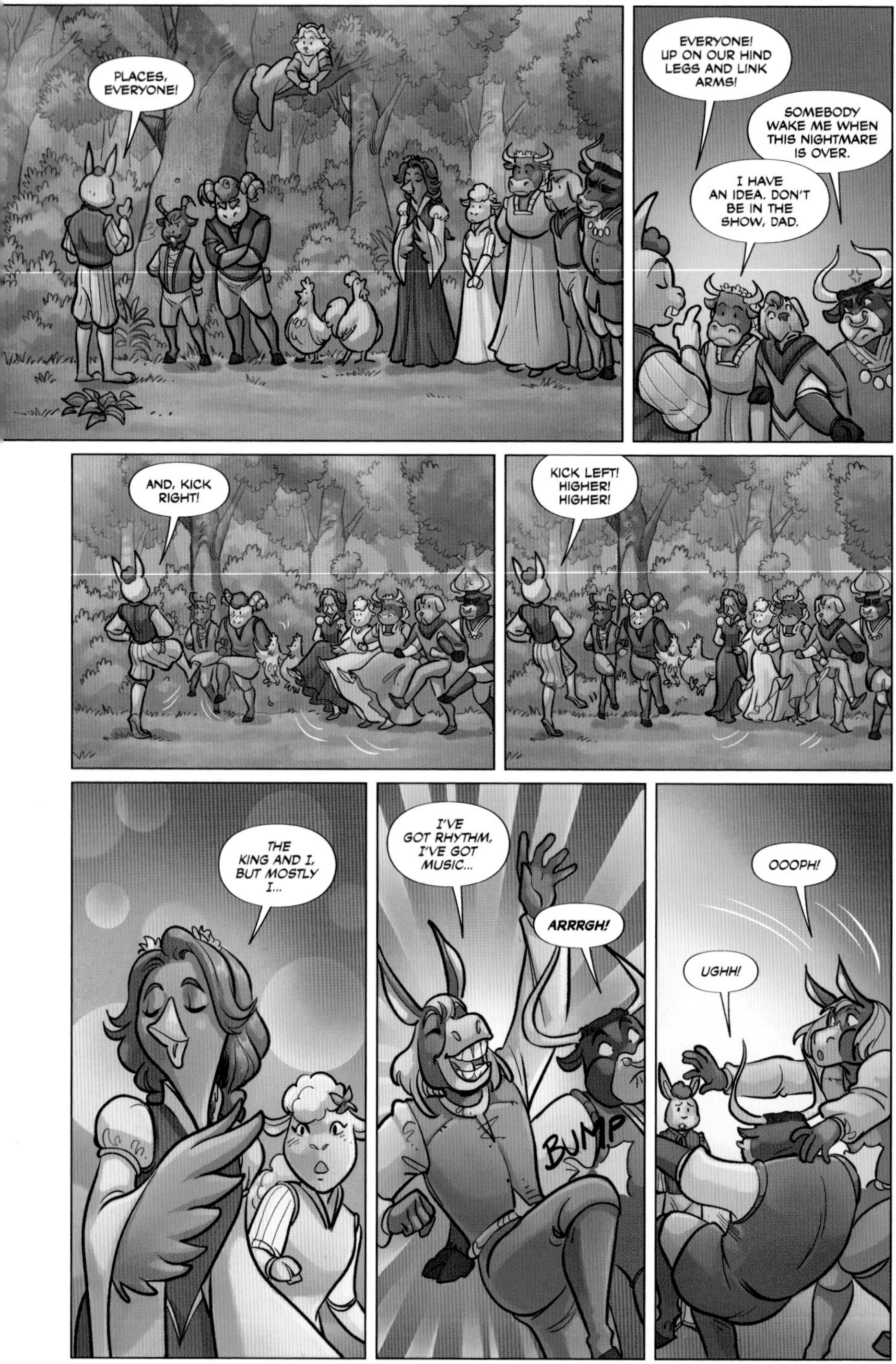
PLACES, EVERYONE!
EVERYONE! UP ON OUR HIND LEGS AND LINK ARMS!
SOMEBODY WAKE ME WHEN THIS NIGHTMARE IS OVER.
I HAVE AN IDEA. DON'T BE IN THE SHOW, DAD.
AND, KICK RIGHT!
KICK LEFT! HIGHER! HIGHER!
THE KING AND I, BUT MOSTLY I...
I'VE GOT RHYTHM, I'VE GOT MUSIC...
ARRRGH!
BUMP
OOOPH!
UGHH!

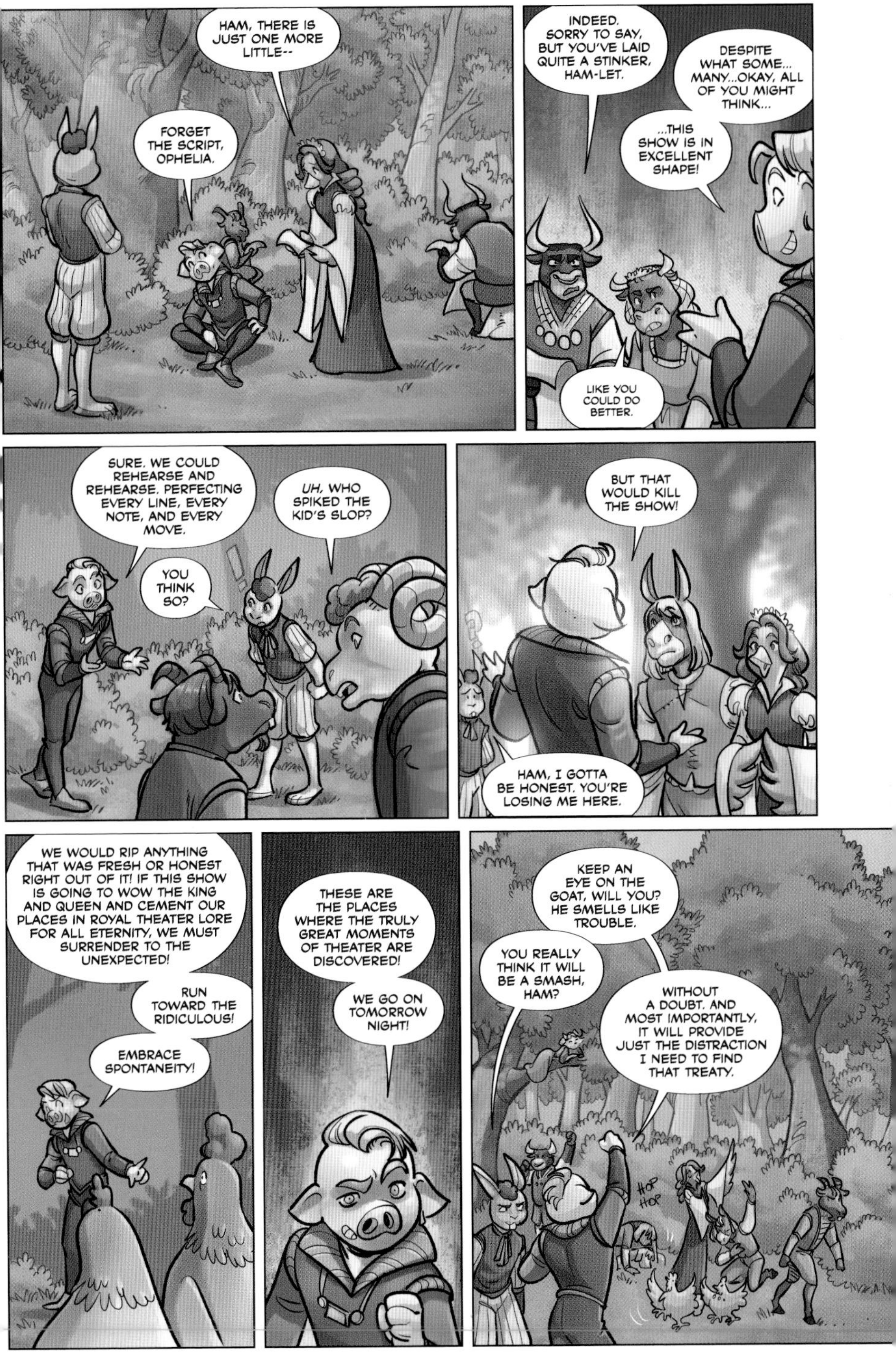
HAM, THERE IS JUST ONE MORE LITTLE--
FORGET THE SCRIPT, OPHELIA.
INDEED. SORRY TO SAY, BUT YOU'VE LAID QUITE A STINKER, HAM-LET.
DESPITE WHAT SOME... MANY...OKAY, ALL OF YOU MIGHT THINK...
...THIS SHOW IS IN EXCELLENT SHAPE!
LIKE YOU COULD DO BETTER.
SURE. WE COULD REHEARSE AND REHEARSE. PERFECTING EVERY LINE, EVERY NOTE, AND EVERY MOVE.
YOU THINK SO?
UH, WHO SPIKED THE KID'S SLOP?
BUT THAT WOULD KILL THE SHOW!
HAM, I GOTTA BE HONEST. YOU'RE LOSING ME HERE.
WE WOULD RIP ANYTHING THAT WAS FRESH OR HONEST RIGHT OUT OF IT! IF THIS SHOW IS GOING TO WOW THE KING AND QUEEN AND CEMENT OUR PLACES IN ROYAL THEATER LORE FOR ALL ETERNITY, WE MUST SURRENDER TO THE UNEXPECTED!
RUN TOWARD THE RIDICULOUS!
EMBRACE SPONTANEITY!
THESE ARE THE PLACES WHERE THE TRULY GREAT MOMENTS OF THEATER ARE DISCOVERED!
WE GO ON TOMORROW NIGHT!
KEEP AN EYE ON THE GOAT, WILL YOU? HE SMELLS LIKE TROUBLE.
YOU REALLY THINK IT WILL BE A SMASH, HAM?
WITHOUT A DOUBT. AND MOST IMPORTANTLY, IT WILL PROVIDE JUST THE DISTRACTION I NEED TO FIND THAT TREATY.
HOP HOP

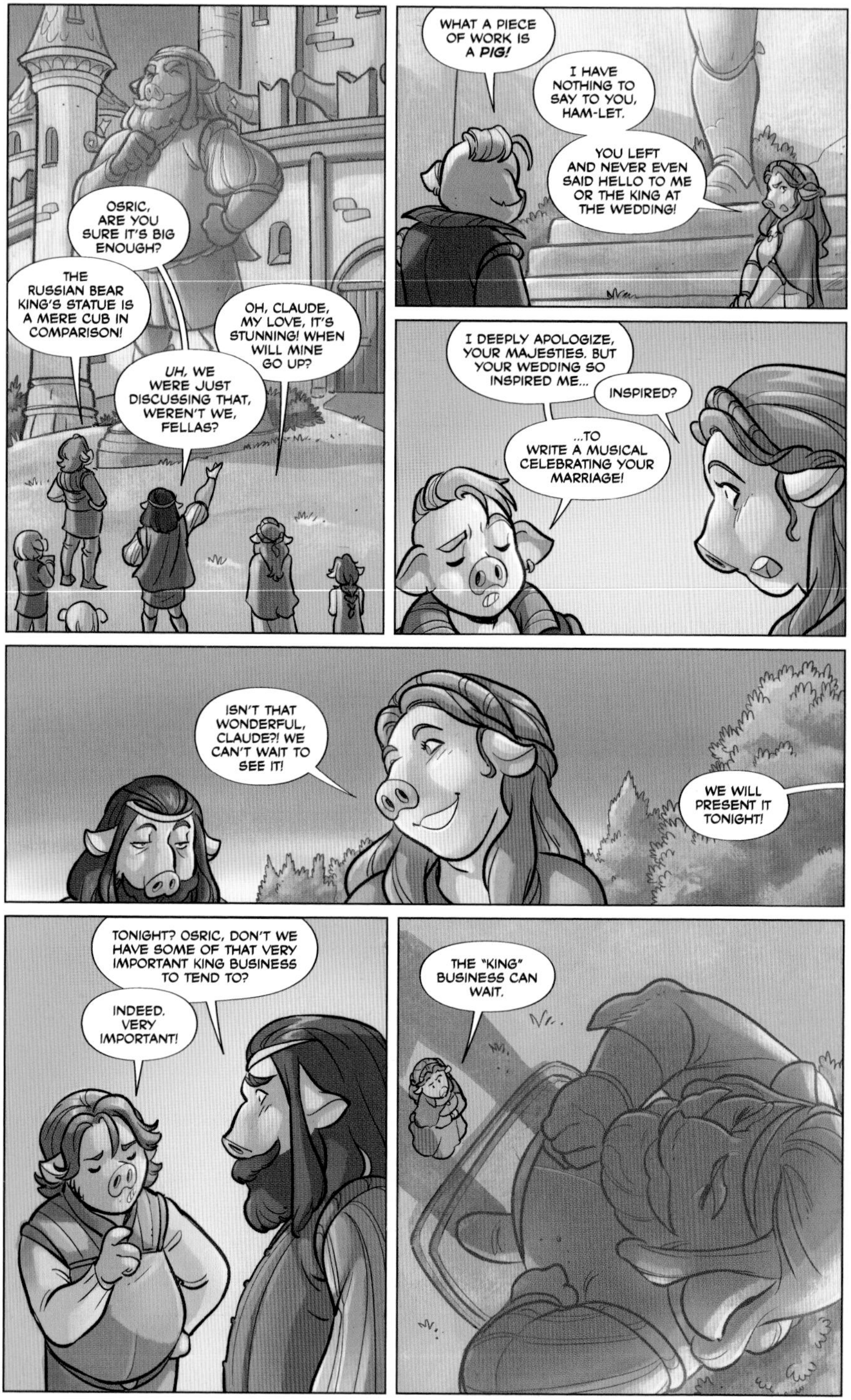
OSRIC, ARE YOU SURE IT'S BIG ENOUGH?
THE RUSSIAN BEAR KING'S STATUE IS A MERE CUB IN COMPARISON!
OH, CLAUDE, MY LOVE, IT'S STUNNING! WHEN WILL MINE GO UP?
UH, WE WERE JUST DISCUSSING THAT, WEREN'T WE, FELLAS?
WHAT A PIECE OF WORK IS A *PIG!*
I HAVE NOTHING TO SAY TO YOU, HAM-LET.
YOU LEFT AND NEVER EVEN SAID HELLO TO ME OR THE KING AT THE WEDDING!
I DEEPLY APOLOGIZE, YOUR MAJESTIES. BUT YOUR WEDDING SO INSPIRED ME...
INSPIRED?
...TO WRITE A MUSICAL CELEBRATING YOUR MARRIAGE!
ISN'T THAT WONDERFUL, CLAUDE?! WE CAN'T WAIT TO SEE IT!
WE WILL PRESENT IT TONIGHT!
TONIGHT? OSRIC, DON'T WE HAVE SOME OF THAT VERY IMPORTANT KING BUSINESS TO TEND TO?
INDEED. VERY IMPORTANT!
THE "KING" BUSINESS CAN WAIT.

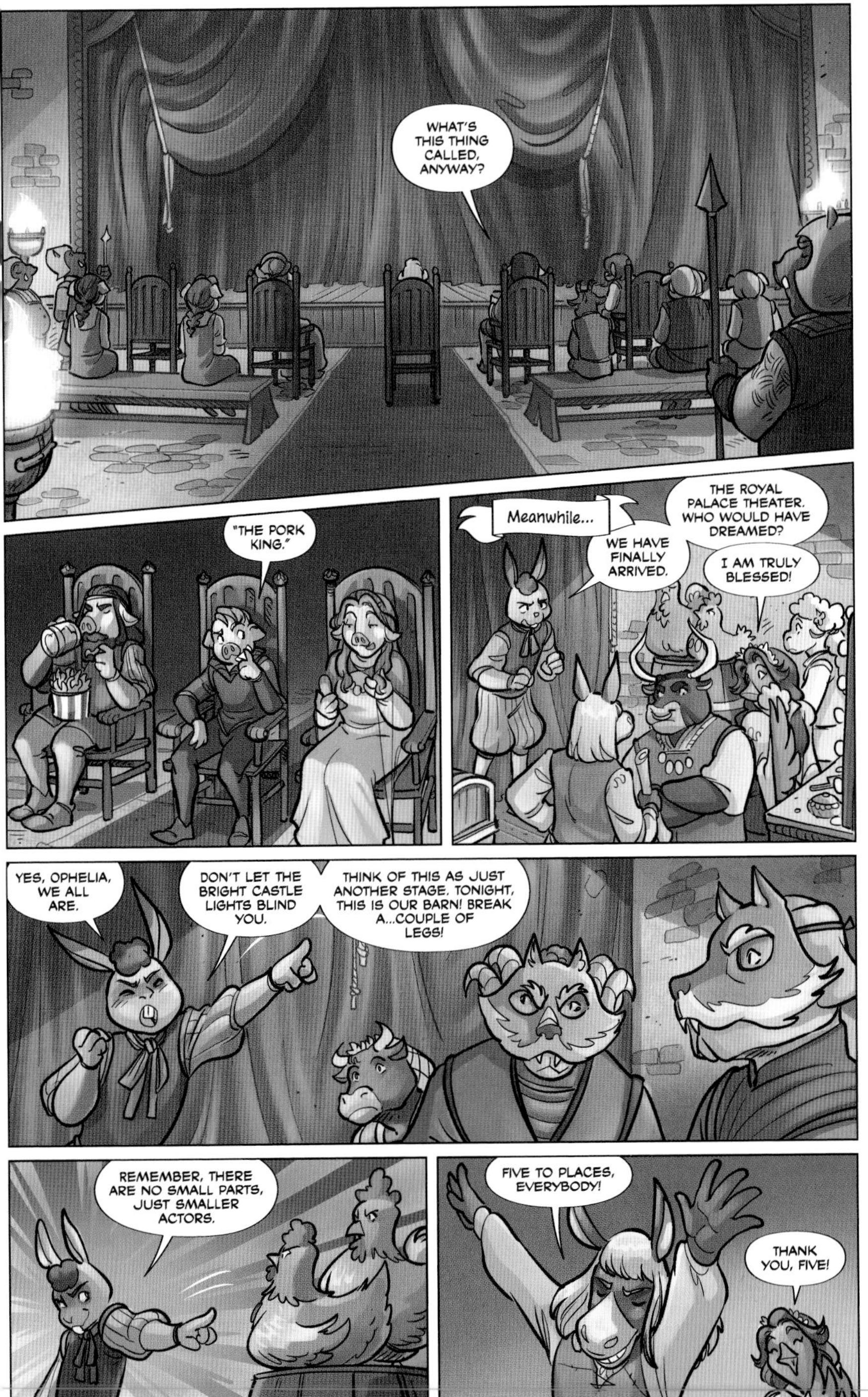
WHAT'S THIS THING CALLED, ANYWAY?
"THE PORK KING."
Meanwhile...
WE HAVE FINALLY ARRIVED.
THE ROYAL PALACE THEATER. WHO WOULD HAVE DREAMED?
I AM TRULY BLESSED!
YES, OPHELIA, WE ALL ARE.
DON'T LET THE BRIGHT CASTLE LIGHTS BLIND YOU.
THINK OF THIS AS JUST ANOTHER STAGE. TONIGHT, THIS IS OUR BARN! BREAK A...COUPLE OF LEGS!
REMEMBER, THERE ARE NO SMALL PARTS, JUST SMALLER ACTORS.
FIVE TO PLACES, EVERYBODY!
THANK YOU, FIVE!

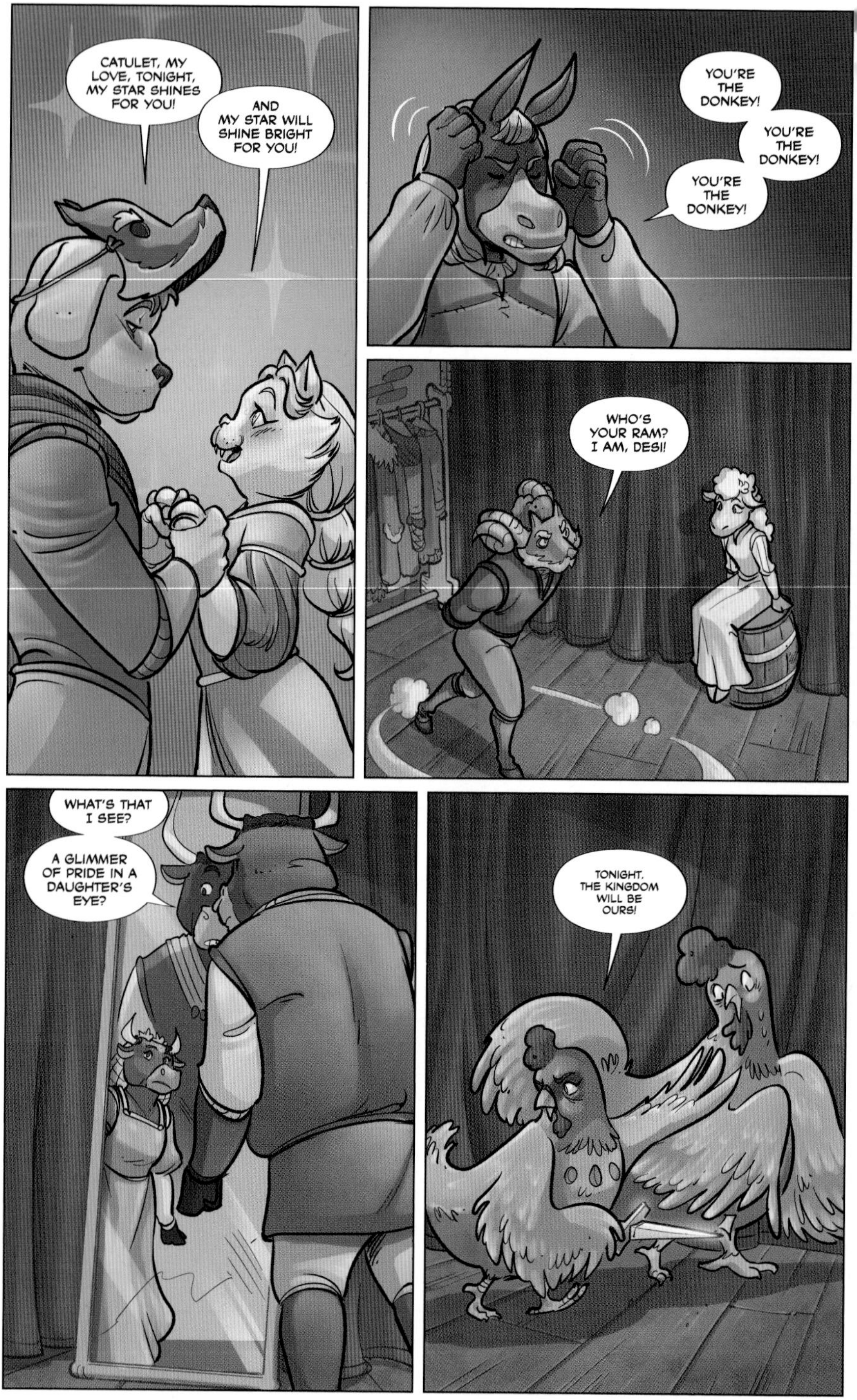
CATULET, MY LOVE, TONIGHT, MY STAR SHINES FOR YOU!
AND MY STAR WILL SHINE BRIGHT FOR YOU!
YOU'RE THE DONKEY!
YOU'RE THE DONKEY!
YOU'RE THE DONKEY!
WHO'S YOUR RAM? I AM, DESI!
WHAT'S THAT I SEE?
A GLIMMER OF PRIDE IN A DAUGHTER'S EYE?
TONIGHT, THE KINGDOM WILL BE OURS!

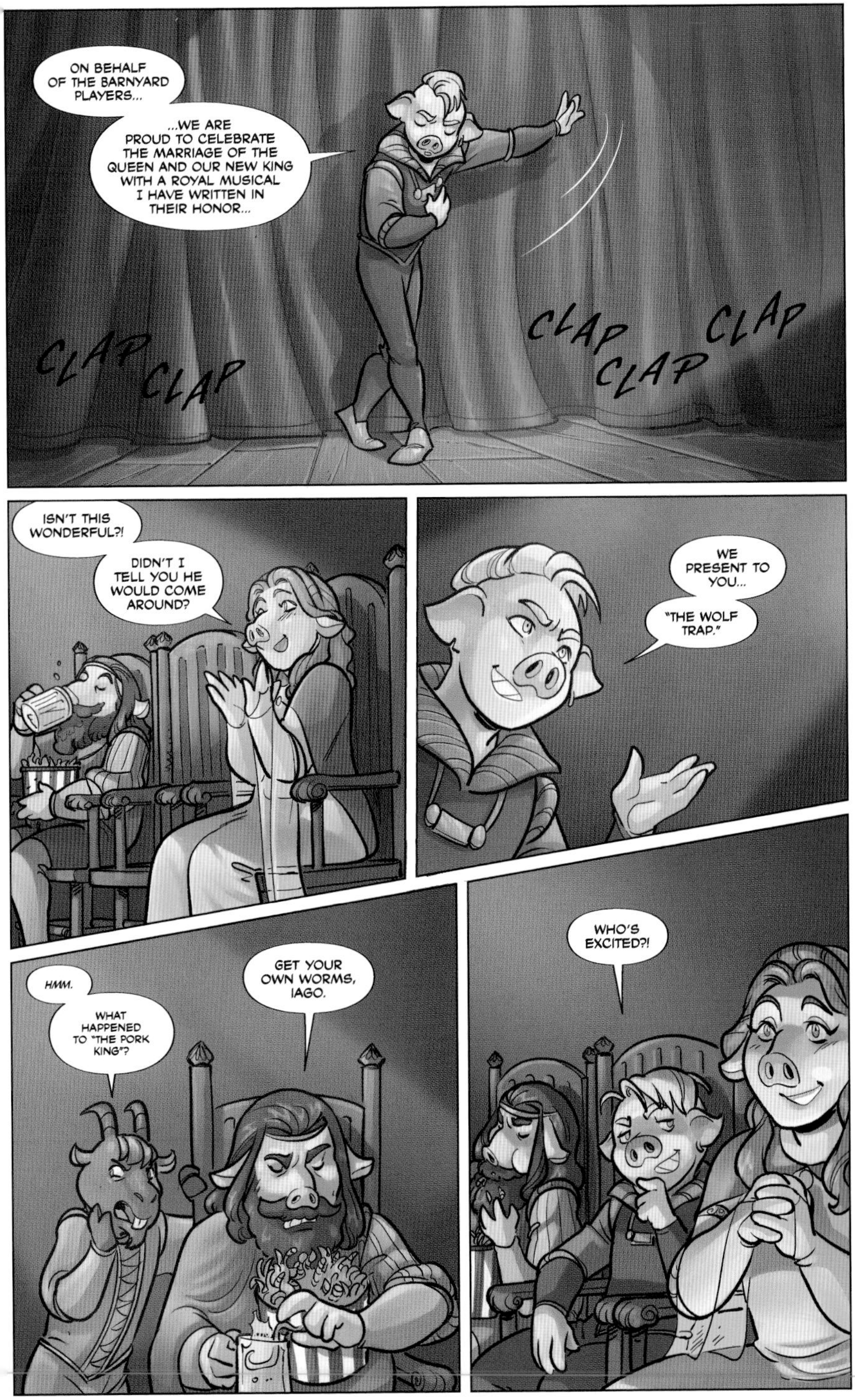
ON BEHALF OF THE BARNYARD PLAYERS...
...WE ARE PROUD TO CELEBRATE THE MARRIAGE OF THE QUEEN AND OUR NEW KING WITH A ROYAL MUSICAL I HAVE WRITTEN IN THEIR HONOR...
CLAP CLAP
CLAP CLAP CLAP
ISN'T THIS WONDERFUL?!
DIDN'T I TELL YOU HE WOULD COME AROUND?
WE PRESENT TO YOU...
"THE WOLF TRAP."
HMM.
WHAT HAPPENED TO "THE PORK KING"?
GET YOUR OWN WORMS, IAGO.
WHO'S EXCITED?!

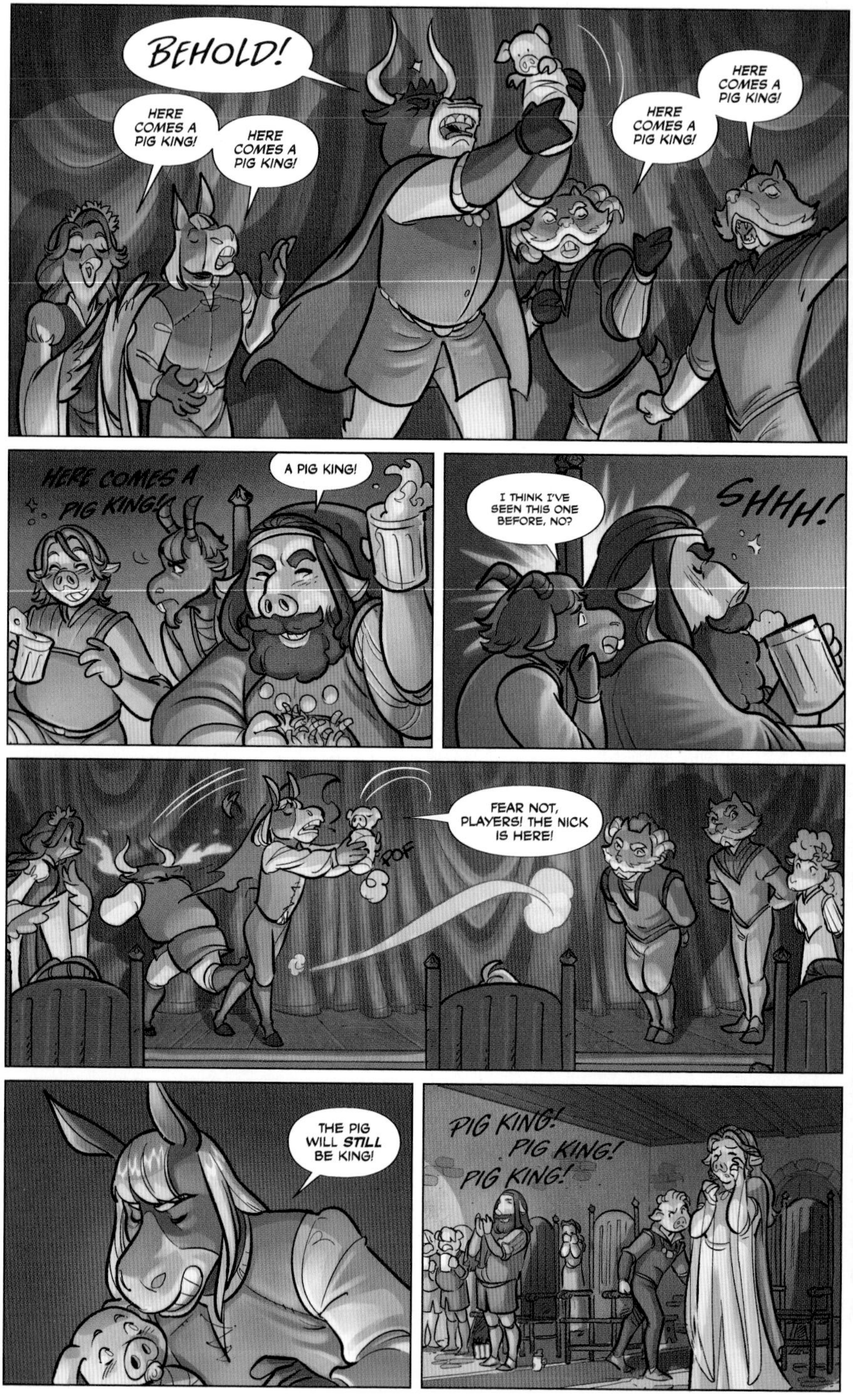
BEHOLD!
HERE COMES A PIG KING!
HERE COMES A PIG KING!
HERE COMES A PIG KING!
HERE COMES A PIG KING!
HERE COMES A PIG KING!
A PIG KING!
I THINK I'VE SEEN THIS ONE BEFORE, NO?
SHHH!
FEAR NOT, PLAYERS! THE NICK IS HERE!
POF
THE PIG WILL STILL BE KING!
PIG KING!
PIG KING!
PIG KING!

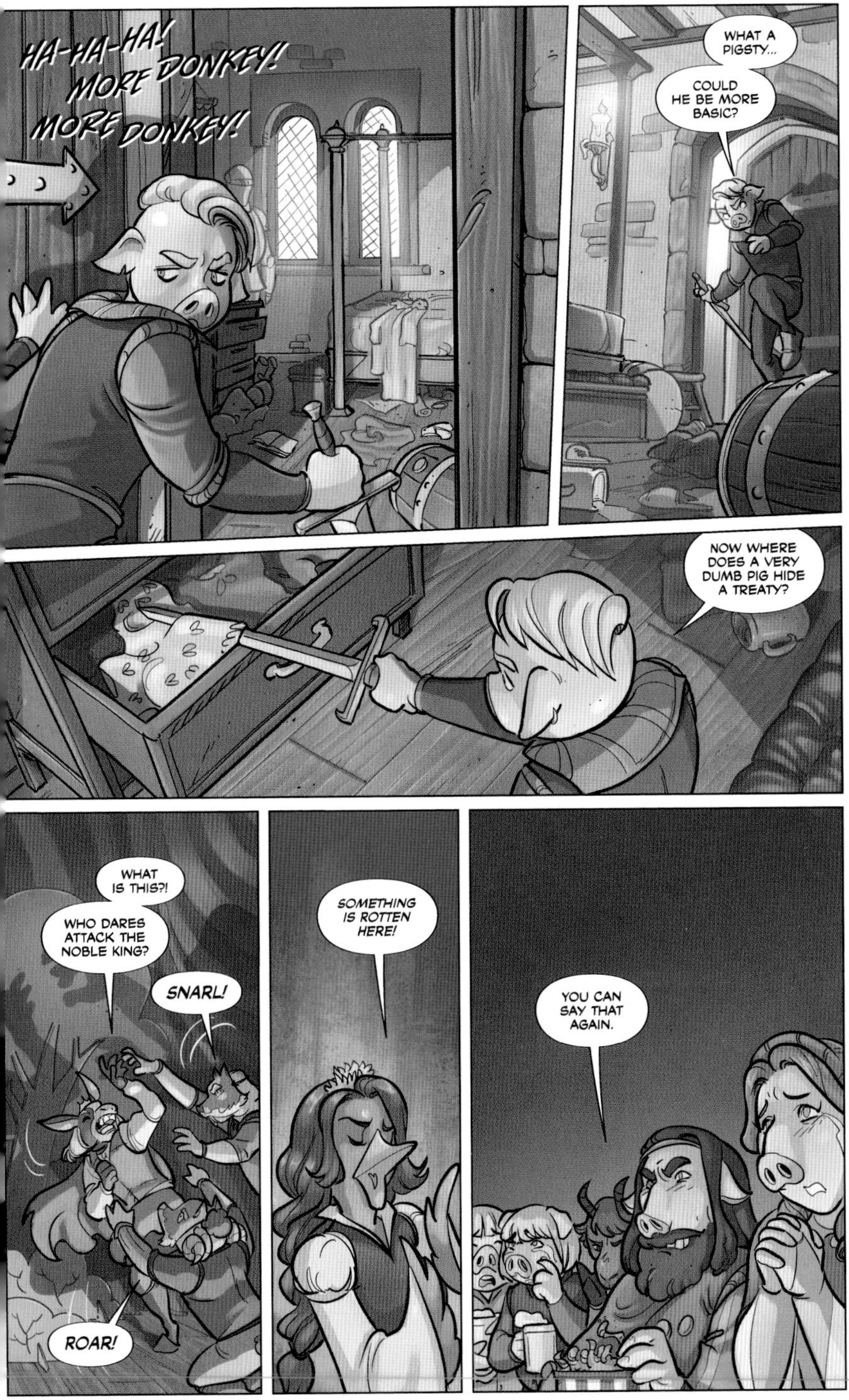
HA-HA-HA!
MORE DONKEY!
MORE DONKEY!
WHAT A PIGSTY...
COULD HE BE MORE BASIC?
NOW WHERE DOES A VERY DUMB PIG HIDE A TREATY?
WHAT IS THIS?!
WHO DARES ATTACK THE NOBLE KING?
SNARL!
ROAR!
SOMETHING IS ROTTEN HERE!
YOU CAN SAY THAT AGAIN.

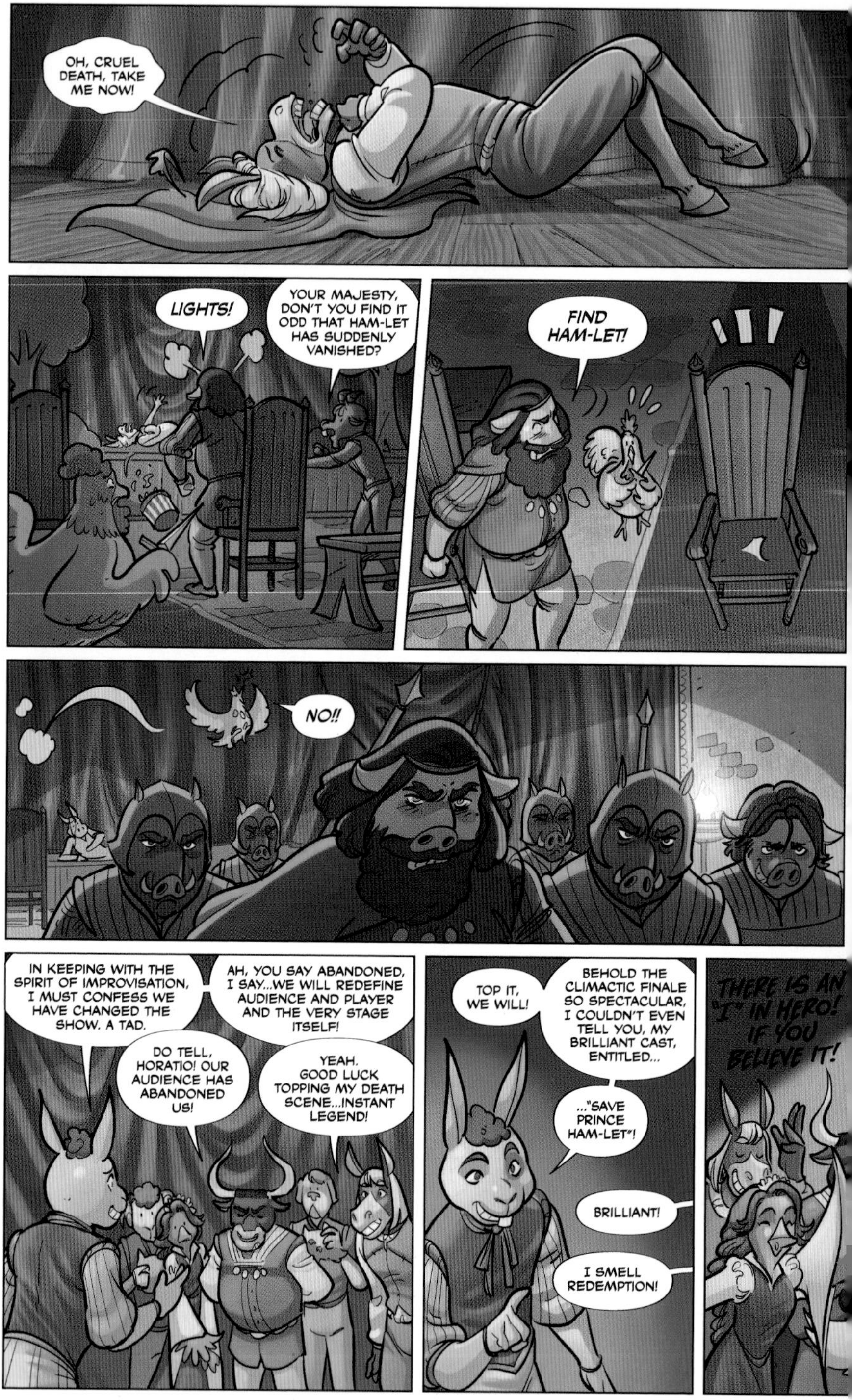

OH, CRUEL DEATH, TAKE ME NOW!
LIGHTS!
YOUR MAJESTY, DON'T YOU FIND IT ODD THAT HAM-LET HAS SUDDENLY VANISHED?
FIND HAM-LET!
NO!!
IN KEEPING WITH THE SPIRIT OF IMPROVISATION, I MUST CONFESS WE HAVE CHANGED THE SHOW. A TAD.
DO TELL, HORATIO! OUR AUDIENCE HAS ABANDONED US!
AH, YOU SAY ABANDONED, I SAY...WE WILL REDEFINE AUDIENCE AND PLAYER AND THE VERY STAGE ITSELF!
YEAH. GOOD LUCK TOPPING MY DEATH SCENE...INSTANT LEGEND!
TOP IT, WE WILL!
BEHOLD THE CLIMACTIC FINALE SO SPECTACULAR, I COULDN'T EVEN TELL YOU, MY BRILLIANT CAST, ENTITLED...
..."SAVE PRINCE HAM-LET"!
BRILLIANT!
I SMELL REDEMPTION!
THERE IS AN "I" IN HERO! IF YOU BELIEVE IT!

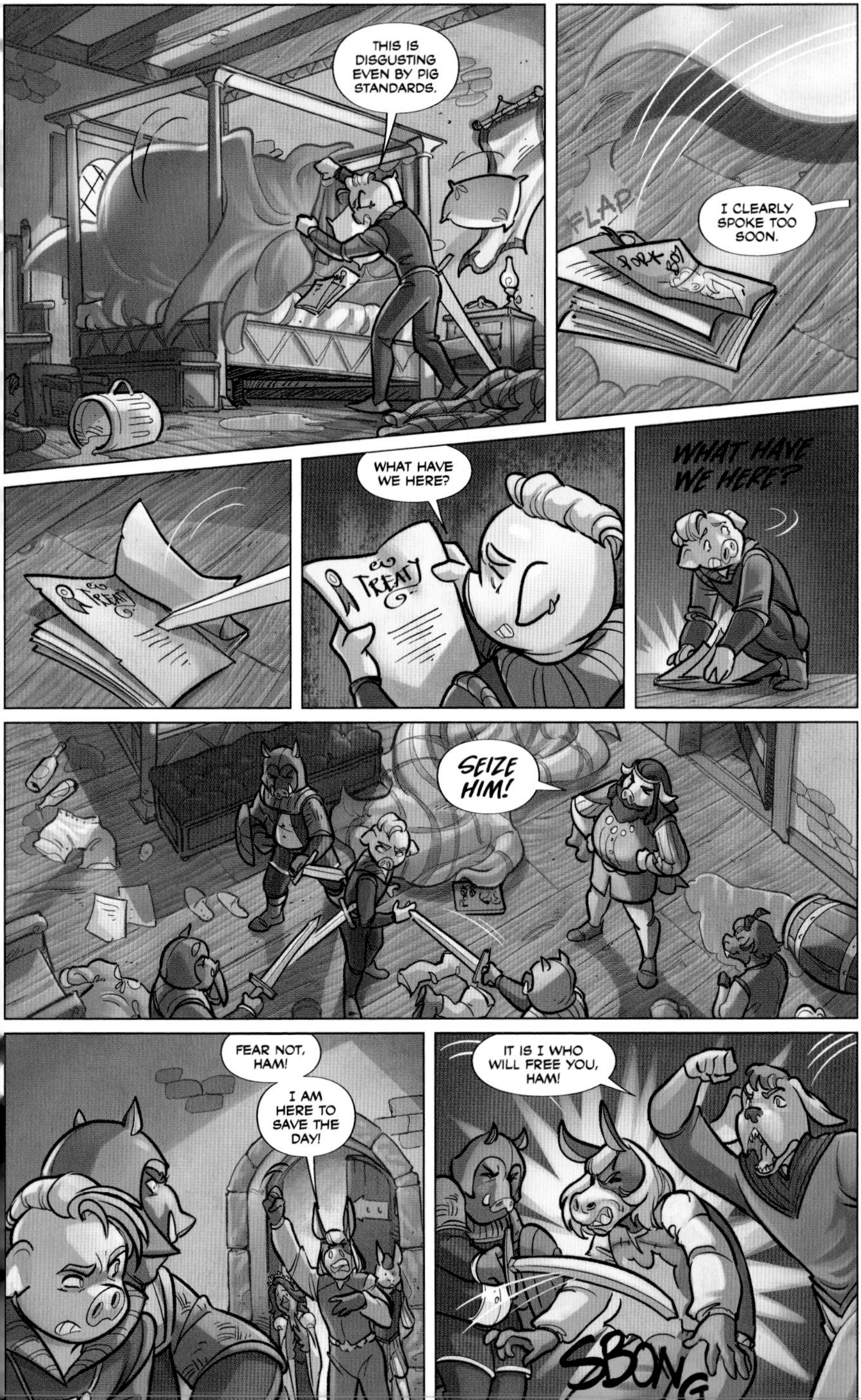
THIS IS DISGUSTING EVEN BY PIG STANDARDS.
FLAP
PORK BOY
I CLEARLY SPOKE TOO SOON.
TREATY
WHAT HAVE WE HERE?
TREATY
WHAT HAVE WE HERE?
SEIZE HIM!
FEAR NOT, HAM!
I AM HERE TO SAVE THE DAY!
IT IS I WHO WILL FREE YOU, HAM!
SBONG

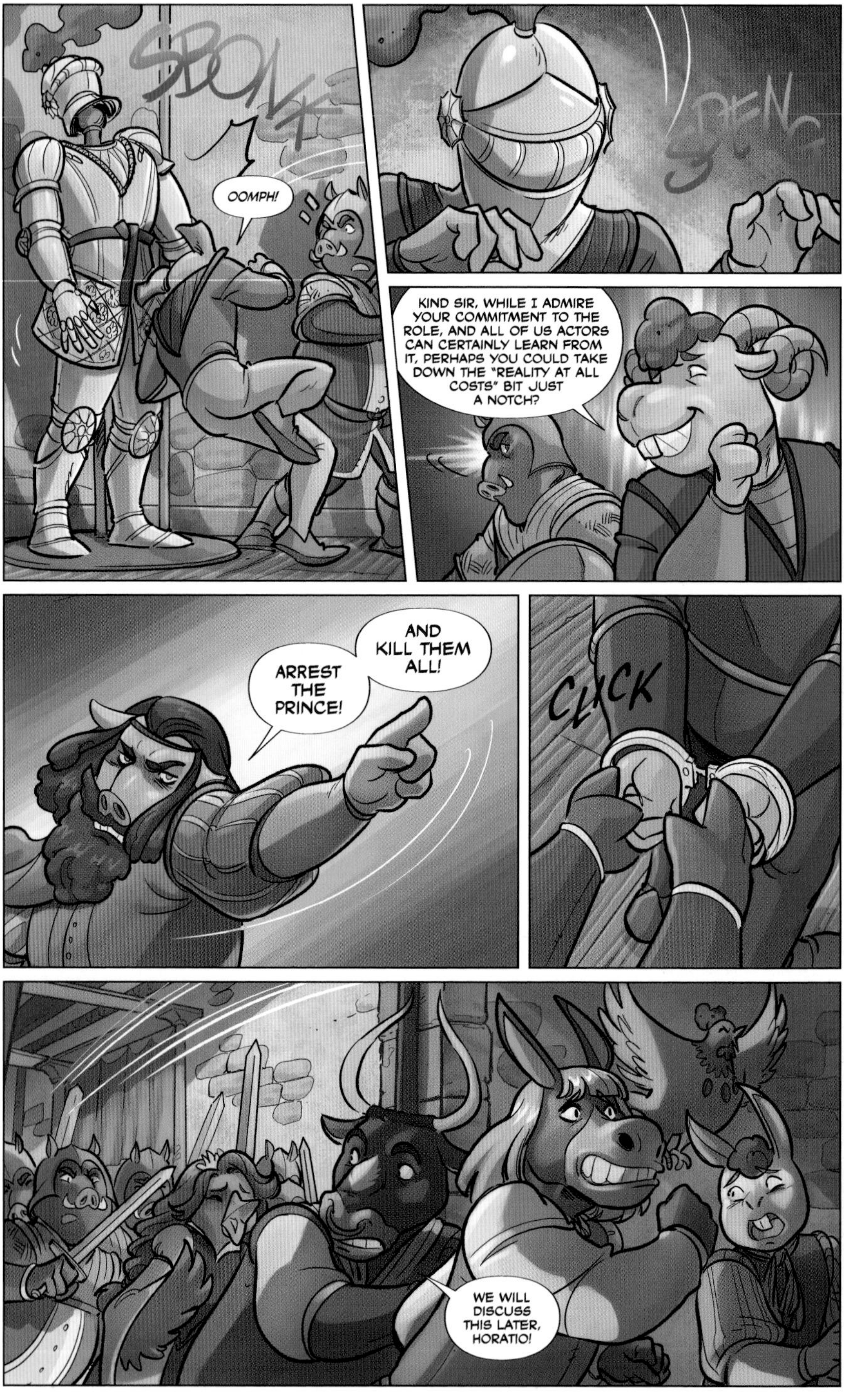
SBONK
OOMPH!
DENG
KIND SIR, WHILE I ADMIRE YOUR COMMITMENT TO THE ROLE, AND ALL OF US ACTORS CAN CERTAINLY LEARN FROM IT, PERHAPS YOU COULD TAKE DOWN THE "REALITY AT ALL COSTS" BIT JUST A NOTCH?
ARREST THE PRINCE!
AND KILL THEM ALL!
CLICK
WE WILL DISCUSS THIS LATER, HORATIO!

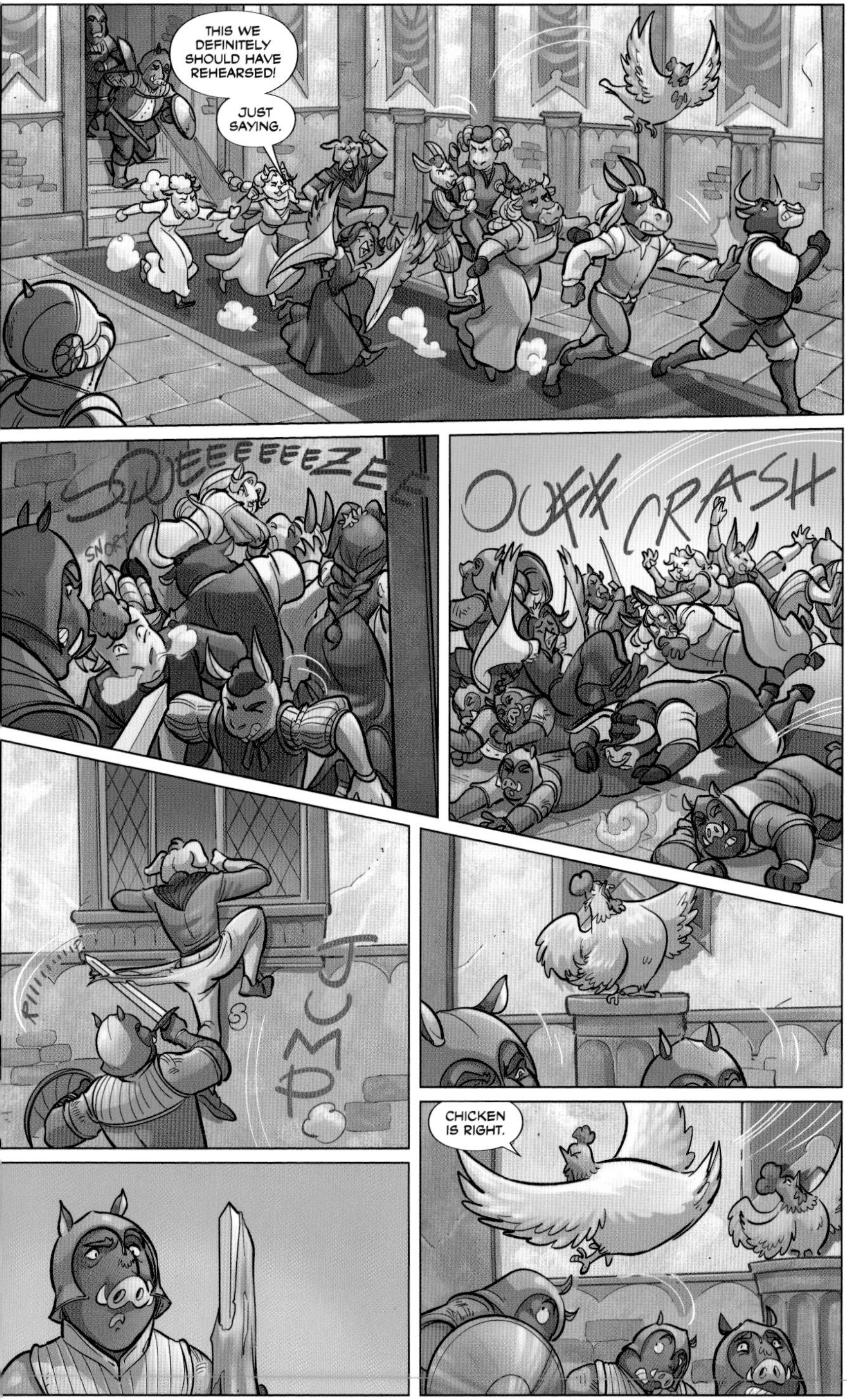
THIS WE DEFINITELY SHOULD HAVE REHEARSED!
JUST SAYING.
SQUEEEEEEEZE
SNORT
OUFF
CRASH
RIIIIP
JUMP
CHICKEN IS RIGHT.

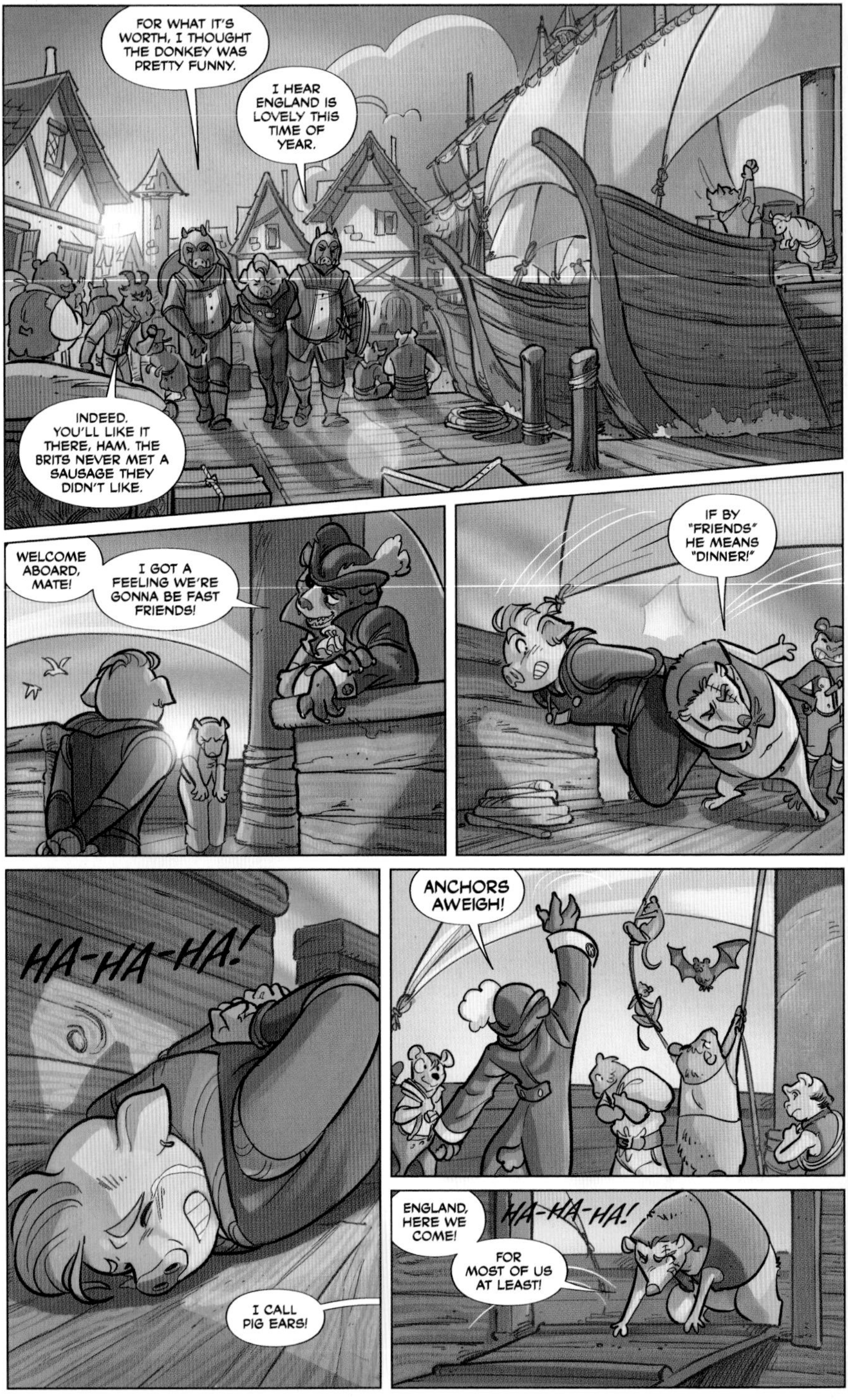
FOR WHAT IT'S WORTH, I THOUGHT THE DONKEY WAS PRETTY FUNNY.
I HEAR ENGLAND IS LOVELY THIS TIME OF YEAR.
INDEED. YOU'LL LIKE IT THERE, HAM. THE BRITS NEVER MET A SAUSAGE THEY DIDN'T LIKE.
WELCOME ABOARD, MATE!
I GOT A FEELING WE'RE GONNA BE FAST FRIENDS!
IF BY "FRIENDS" HE MEANS "DINNER!"
HA-HA-HA!
I CALL PIG EARS!
ANCHORS AWEIGH!
ENGLAND, HERE WE COME!
HA-HA-HA!
FOR MOST OF US AT LEAST!

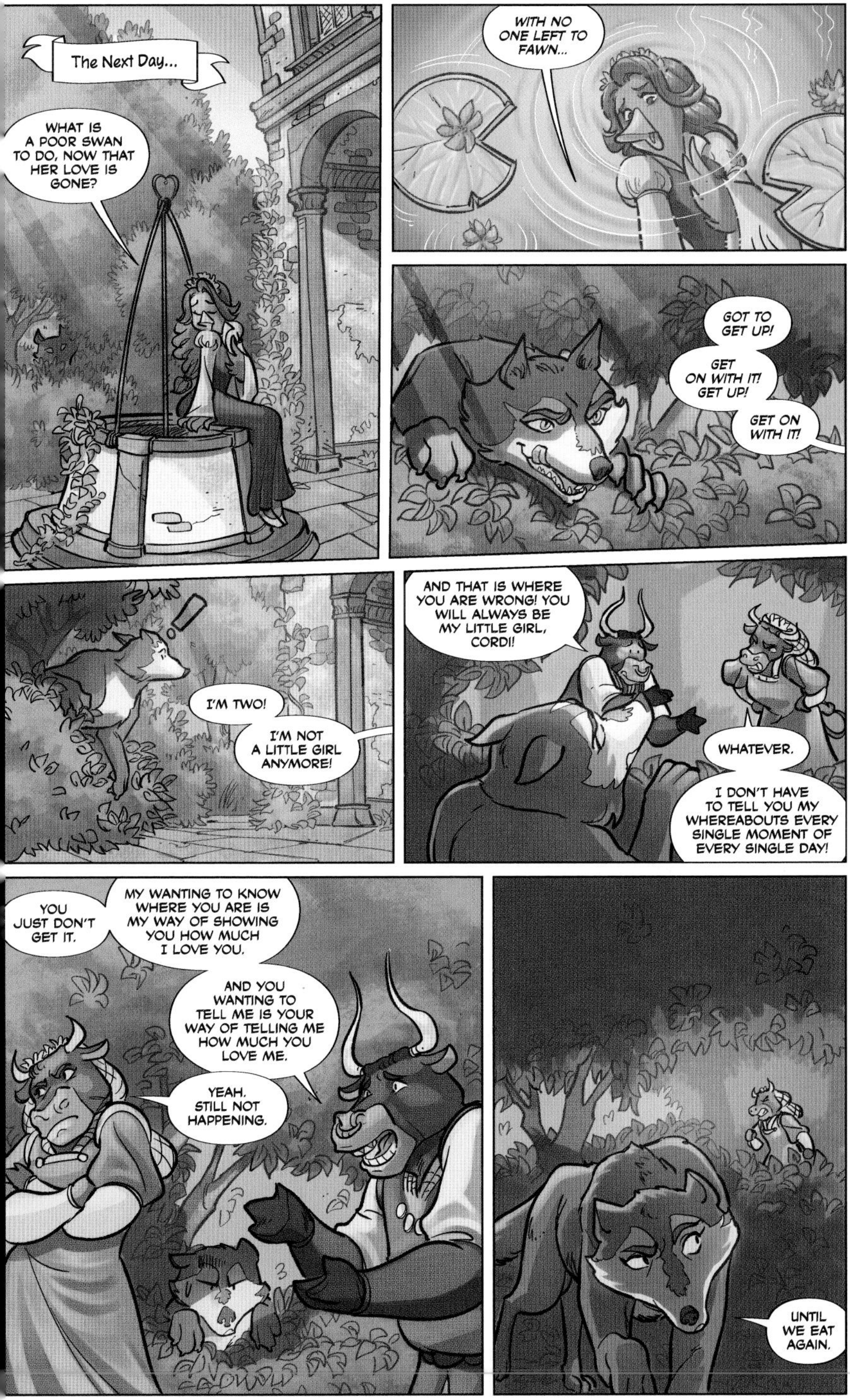
The Next Day...
WHAT IS A POOR SWAN TO DO, NOW THAT HER LOVE IS GONE?
WITH NO ONE LEFT TO FAWN...
GOT TO GET UP!
GET ON WITH IT! GET UP!
GET ON WITH IT!
!
I'M TWO!
I'M NOT A LITTLE GIRL ANYMORE!
AND THAT IS WHERE YOU ARE WRONG! YOU WILL ALWAYS BE MY LITTLE GIRL, CORDI!
WHATEVER.
I DON'T HAVE TO TELL YOU MY WHEREABOUTS EVERY SINGLE MOMENT OF EVERY SINGLE DAY!
YOU JUST DON'T GET IT.
MY WANTING TO KNOW WHERE YOU ARE IS MY WAY OF SHOWING YOU HOW MUCH I LOVE YOU.
AND YOU WANTING TO TELL ME IS YOUR WAY OF TELLING ME HOW MUCH YOU LOVE ME.
YEAH. STILL NOT HAPPENING.
UNTIL WE EAT AGAIN.

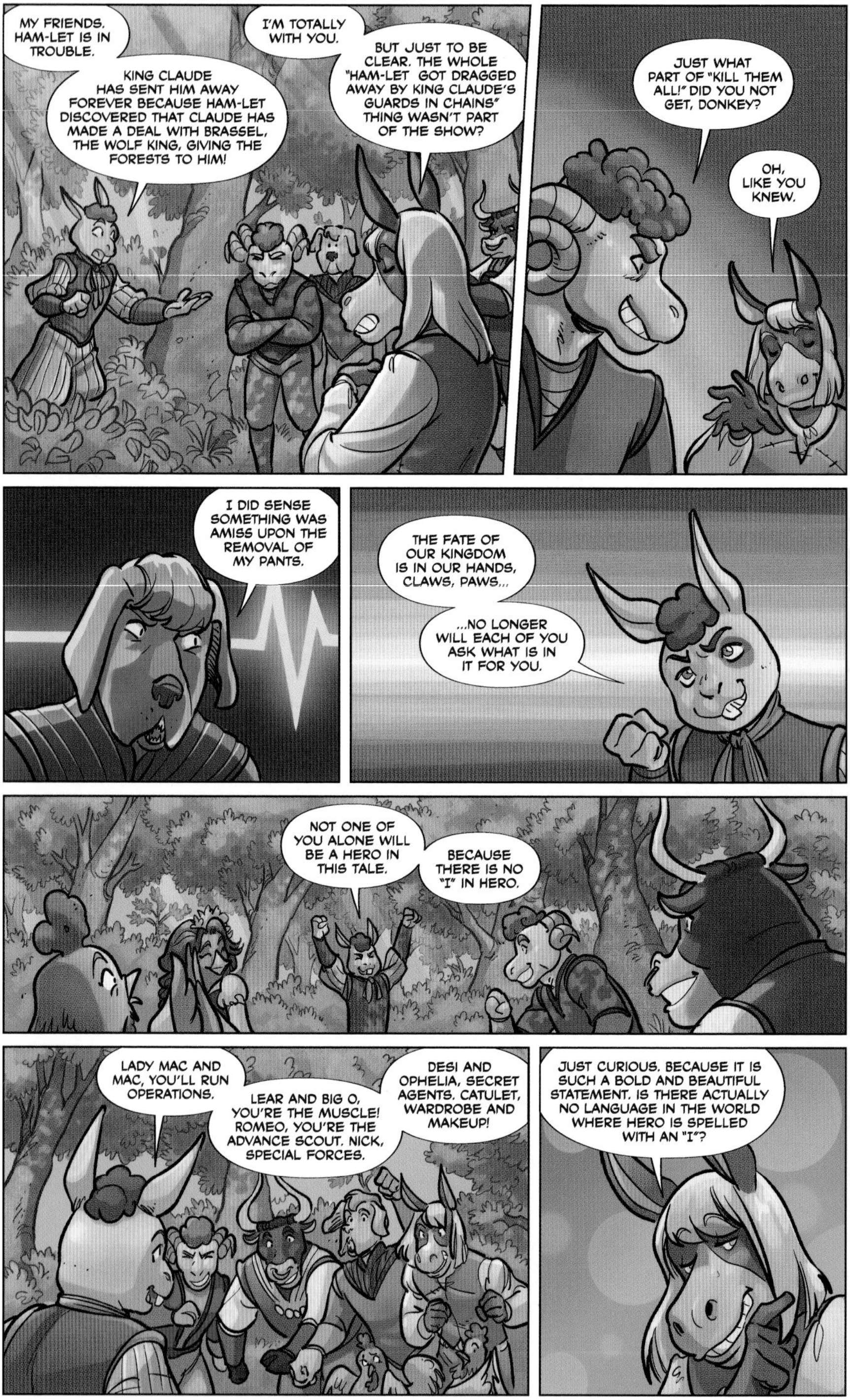
MY FRIENDS. HAM-LET IS IN TROUBLE.
KING CLAUDE HAS SENT HIM AWAY FOREVER BECAUSE HAM-LET DISCOVERED THAT CLAUDE HAS MADE A DEAL WITH BRASSEL, THE WOLF KING, GIVING THE FORESTS TO HIM!
I'M TOTALLY WITH YOU.
BUT JUST TO BE CLEAR. THE WHOLE "HAM-LET GOT DRAGGED AWAY BY KING CLAUDE'S GUARDS IN CHAINS" THING WASN'T PART OF THE SHOW?
JUST WHAT PART OF "KILL THEM ALL!" DID YOU NOT GET, DONKEY?
OH, LIKE YOU KNEW.
I DID SENSE SOMETHING WAS AMISS UPON THE REMOVAL OF MY PANTS.
THE FATE OF OUR KINGDOM IS IN OUR HANDS, CLAWS, PAWS...
...NO LONGER WILL EACH OF YOU ASK WHAT IS IN IT FOR YOU.
NOT ONE OF YOU ALONE WILL BE A HERO IN THIS TALE.
BECAUSE THERE IS NO "I" IN HERO.
LADY MAC AND MAC, YOU'LL RUN OPERATIONS.
LEAR AND BIG O, YOU'RE THE MUSCLE! ROMEO, YOU'RE THE ADVANCE SCOUT. NICK, SPECIAL FORCES.
DESI AND OPHELIA, SECRET AGENTS. CATULET, WARDROBE AND MAKEUP!
JUST CURIOUS. BECAUSE IT IS SUCH A BOLD AND BEAUTIFUL STATEMENT. IS THERE ACTUALLY NO LANGUAGE IN THE WORLD WHERE HERO IS SPELLED WITH AN "I"?

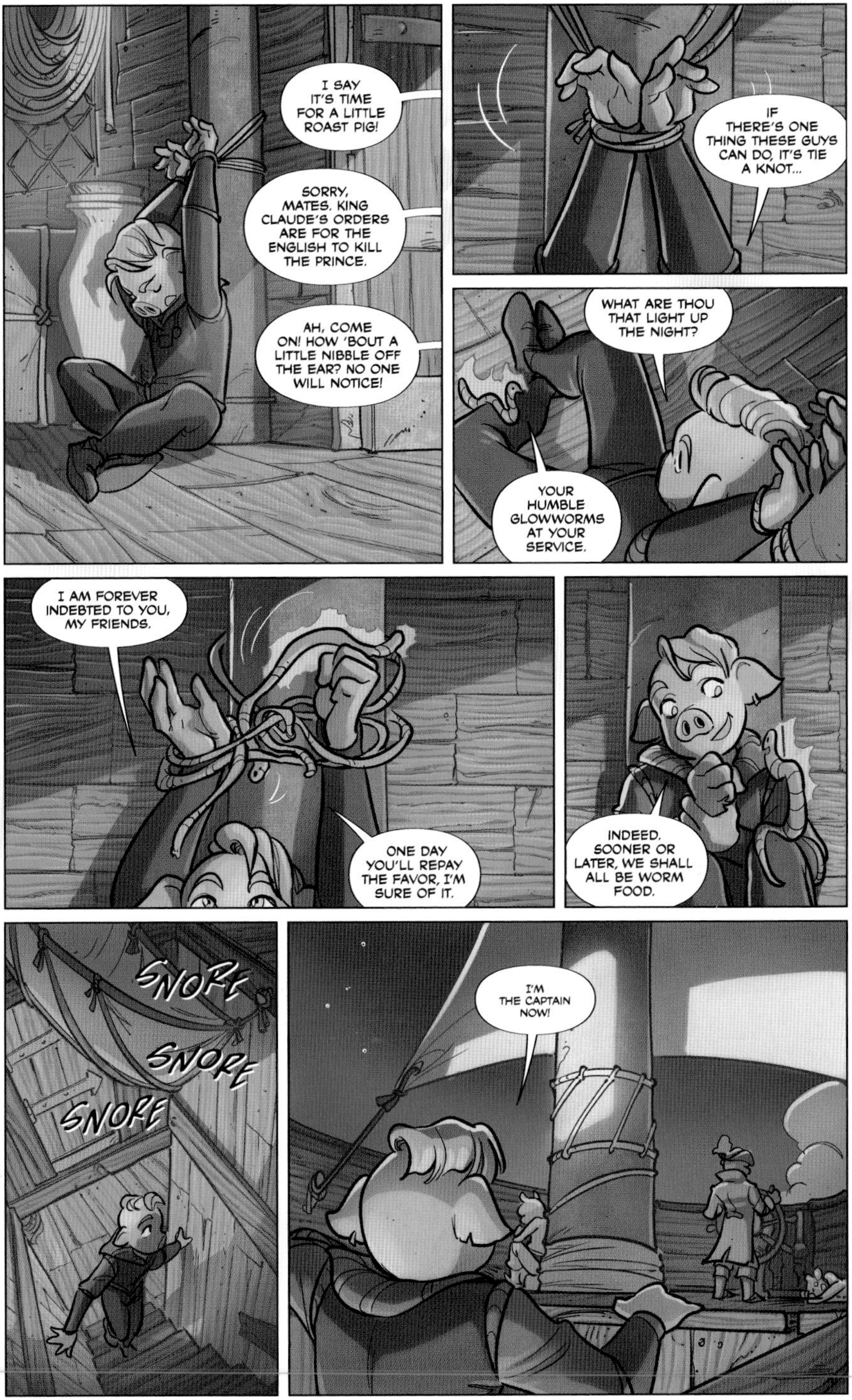
I SAY IT'S TIME FOR A LITTLE ROAST PIG!
SORRY, MATES. KING CLAUDE'S ORDERS ARE FOR THE ENGLISH TO KILL THE PRINCE.
AH, COME ON! HOW 'BOUT A LITTLE NIBBLE OFF THE EAR? NO ONE WILL NOTICE!
IF THERE'S ONE THING THESE GUYS CAN DO, IT'S TIE A KNOT...
WHAT ARE THOU THAT LIGHT UP THE NIGHT?
YOUR HUMBLE GLOWWORMS AT YOUR SERVICE.
I AM FOREVER INDEBTED TO YOU, MY FRIENDS.
ONE DAY YOU'LL REPAY THE FAVOR, I'M SURE OF IT.
INDEED. SOONER OR LATER, WE SHALL ALL BE WORM FOOD.
SNORE
SNORE
SNORE
I'M THE CAPTAIN NOW!

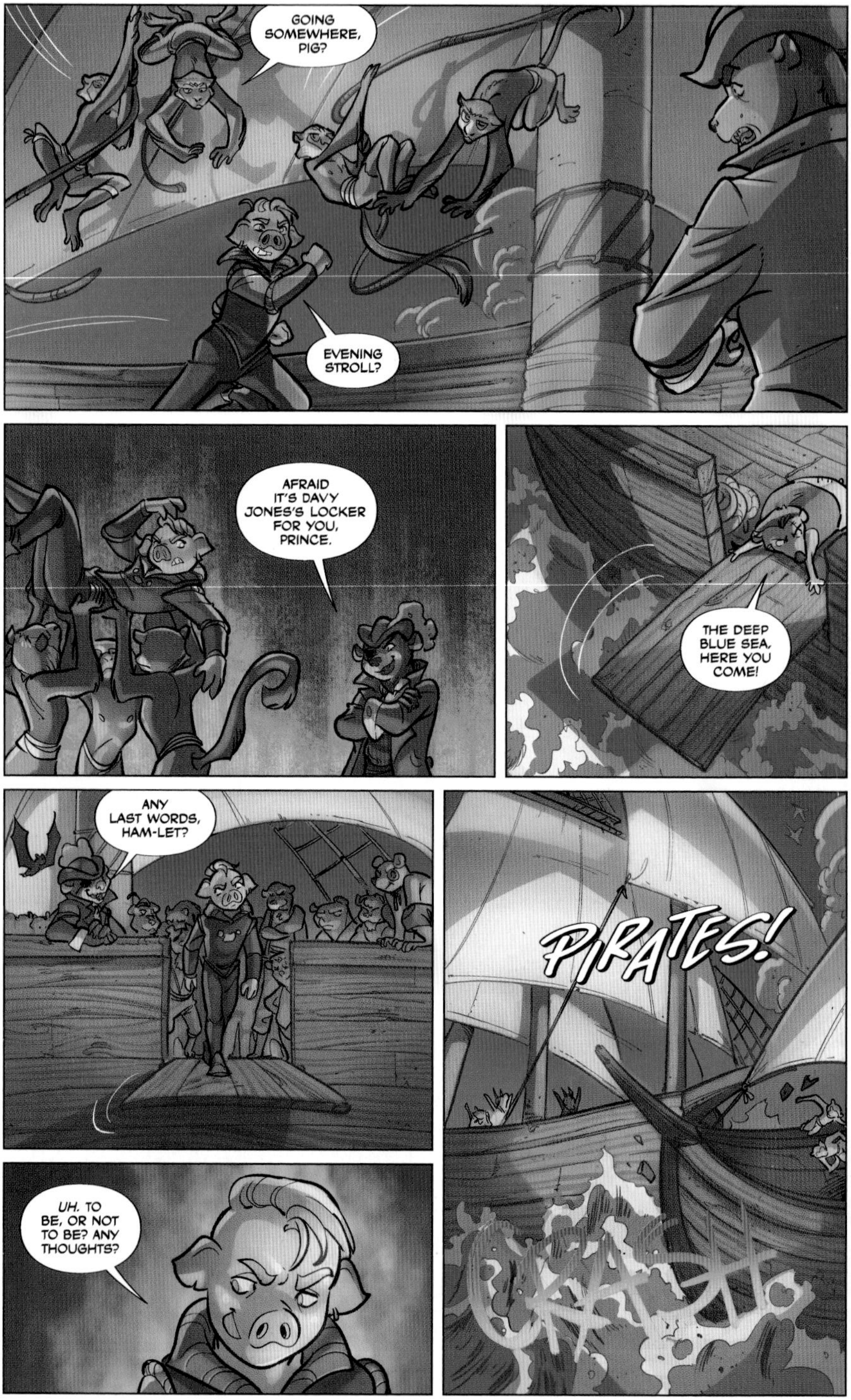
GOING SOMEWHERE, PIG?
EVENING STROLL?
AFRAID IT'S DAVY JONES'S LOCKER FOR YOU, PRINCE.
THE DEEP BLUE SEA, HERE YOU COME!
ANY LAST WORDS, HAM-LET?
UH. TO BE, OR NOT TO BE? ANY THOUGHTS?
PIRATES!

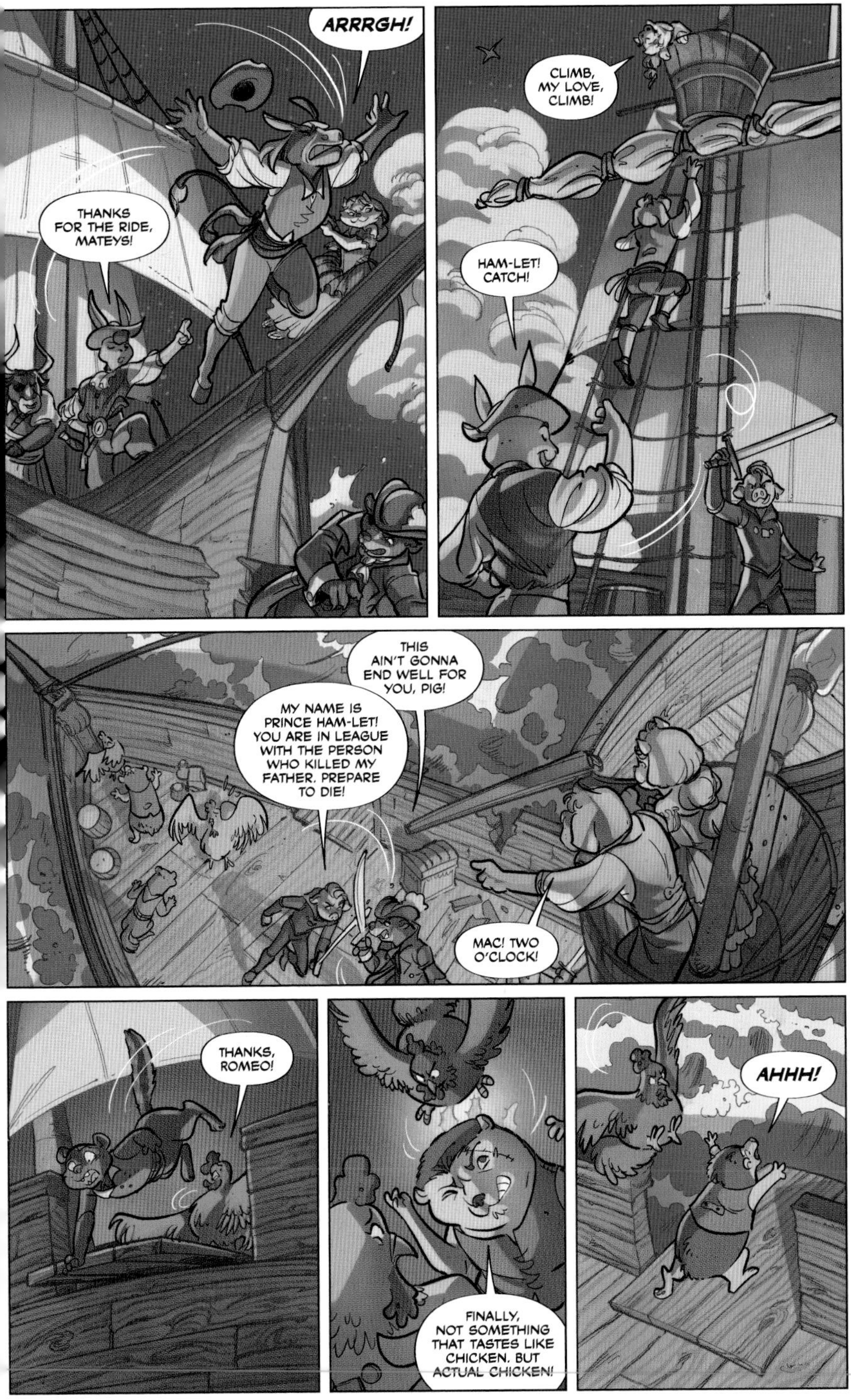
ARRRGH!
THANKS FOR THE RIDE, MATEYS!
CLIMB, MY LOVE, CLIMB!
HAM-LET! CATCH!
THIS AIN'T GONNA END WELL FOR YOU, PIG!
MY NAME IS PRINCE HAM-LET! YOU ARE IN LEAGUE WITH THE PERSON WHO KILLED MY FATHER. PREPARE TO DIE!
MAC! TWO O'CLOCK!
THANKS, ROMEO!
FINALLY, NOT SOMETHING THAT TASTES LIKE CHICKEN, BUT ACTUAL CHICKEN!
AHHH!

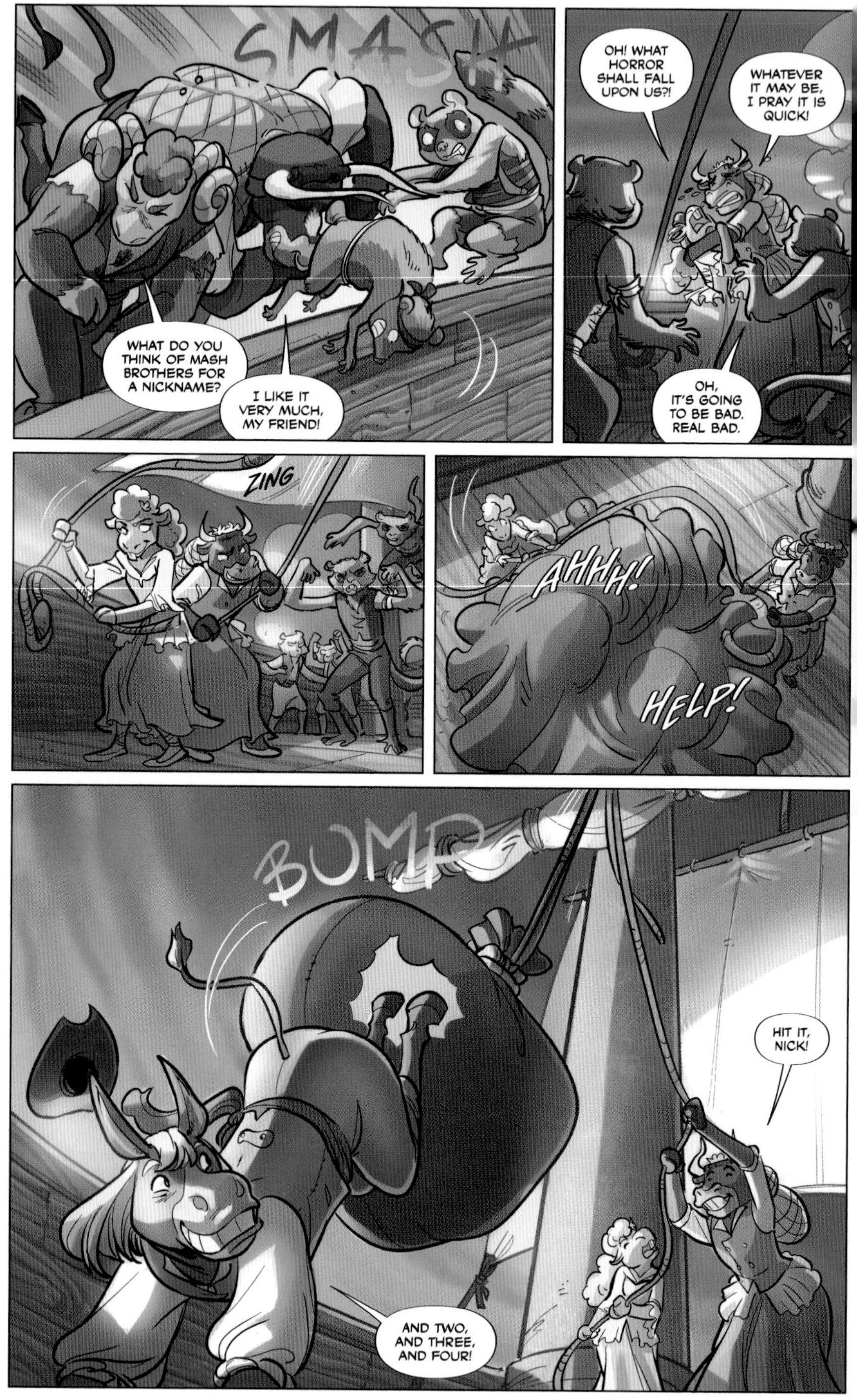
SMASH
WHAT DO YOU THINK OF MASH BROTHERS FOR A NICKNAME?
I LIKE IT VERY MUCH, MY FRIEND!
OH! WHAT HORROR SHALL FALL UPON US?!
WHATEVER IT MAY BE, I PRAY IT IS QUICK!
OH, IT'S GOING TO BE BAD. REAL BAD.
ZING
AHHH!
HELP!
BUMP
HIT IT, NICK!
AND TWO, AND THREE, AND FOUR!

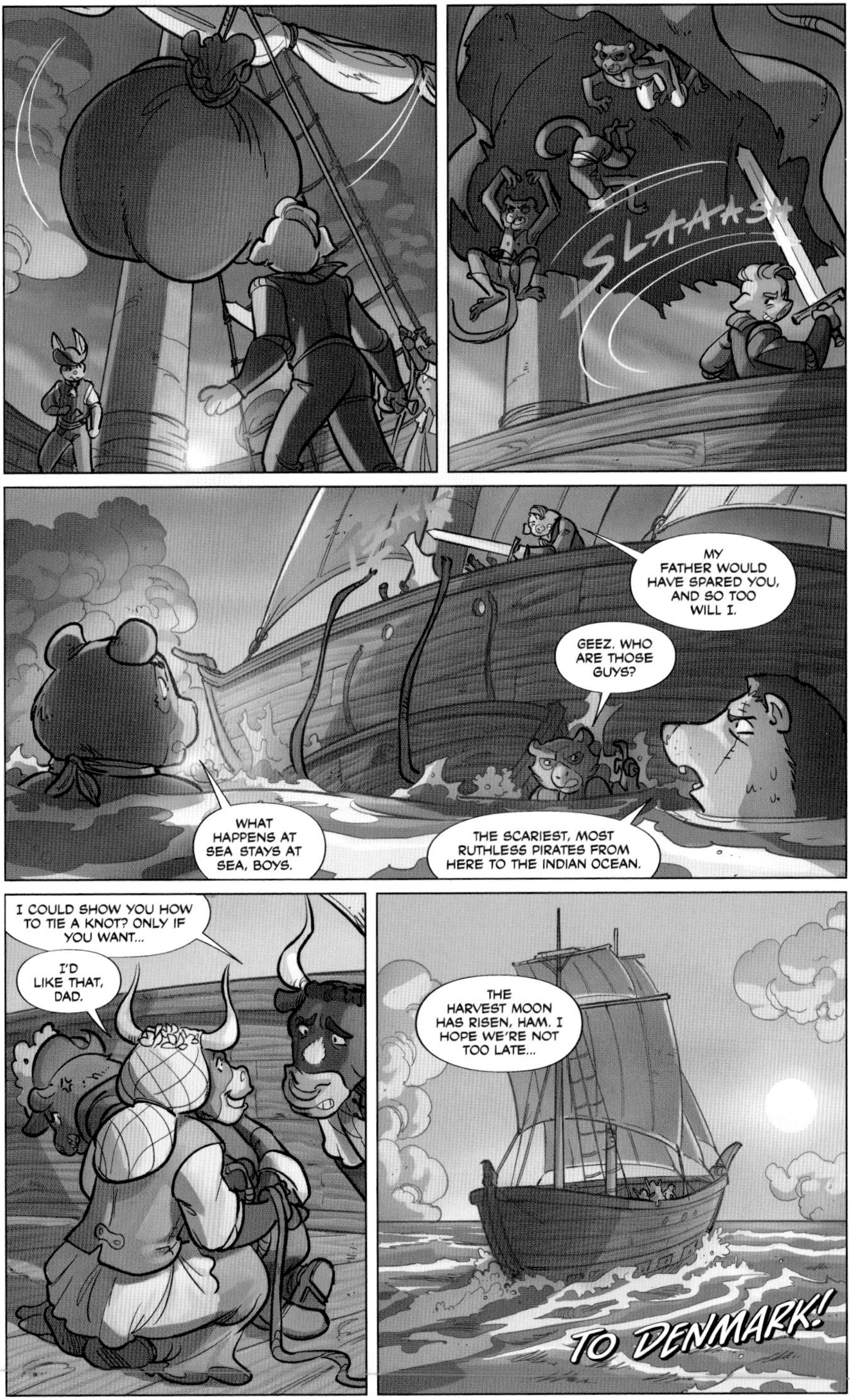
SLAAASH
MY FATHER WOULD HAVE SPARED YOU, AND SO TOO WILL I.
GEEZ. WHO ARE THOSE GUYS?
WHAT HAPPENS AT SEA STAYS AT SEA, BOYS.
THE SCARIEST, MOST RUTHLESS PIRATES FROM HERE TO THE INDIAN OCEAN.
I COULD SHOW YOU HOW TO TIE A KNOT? ONLY IF YOU WANT...
I'D LIKE THAT, DAD.
THE HARVEST MOON HAS RISEN, HAM. I HOPE WE'RE NOT TOO LATE...
TO DENMARK!

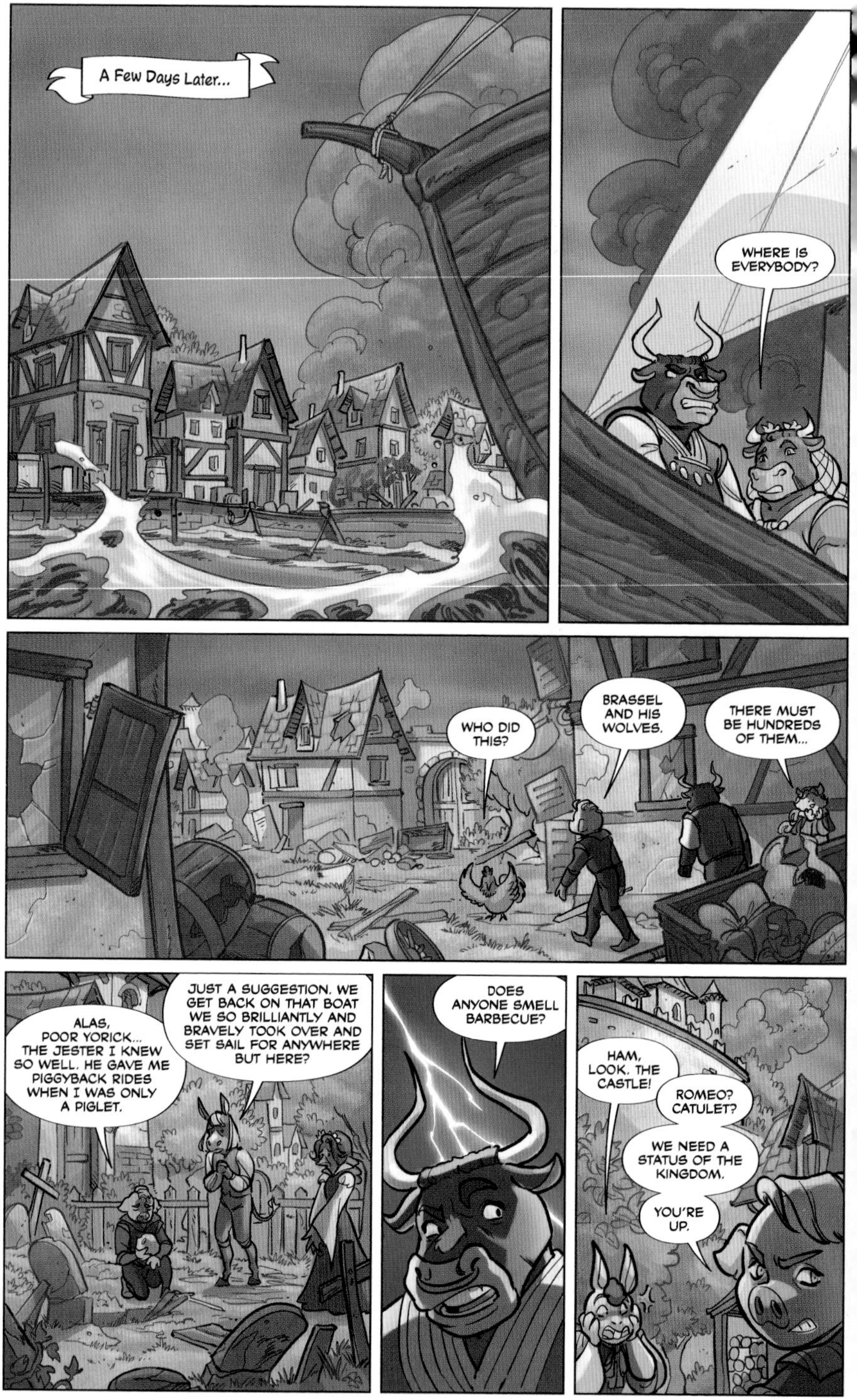
A Few Days Later...
WHERE IS EVERYBODY?
WHO DID THIS?
BRASSEL AND HIS WOLVES.
THERE MUST BE HUNDREDS OF THEM...
ALAS, POOR YORICK... THE JESTER I KNEW SO WELL. HE GAVE ME PIGGYBACK RIDES WHEN I WAS ONLY A PIGLET.
JUST A SUGGESTION. WE GET BACK ON THAT BOAT WE SO BRILLIANTLY AND BRAVELY TOOK OVER AND SET SAIL FOR ANYWHERE BUT HERE?
DOES ANYONE SMELL BARBECUE?
HAM, LOOK, THE CASTLE!
ROMEO? CATULET?
WE NEED A STATUS OF THE KINGDOM.
YOU'RE UP.

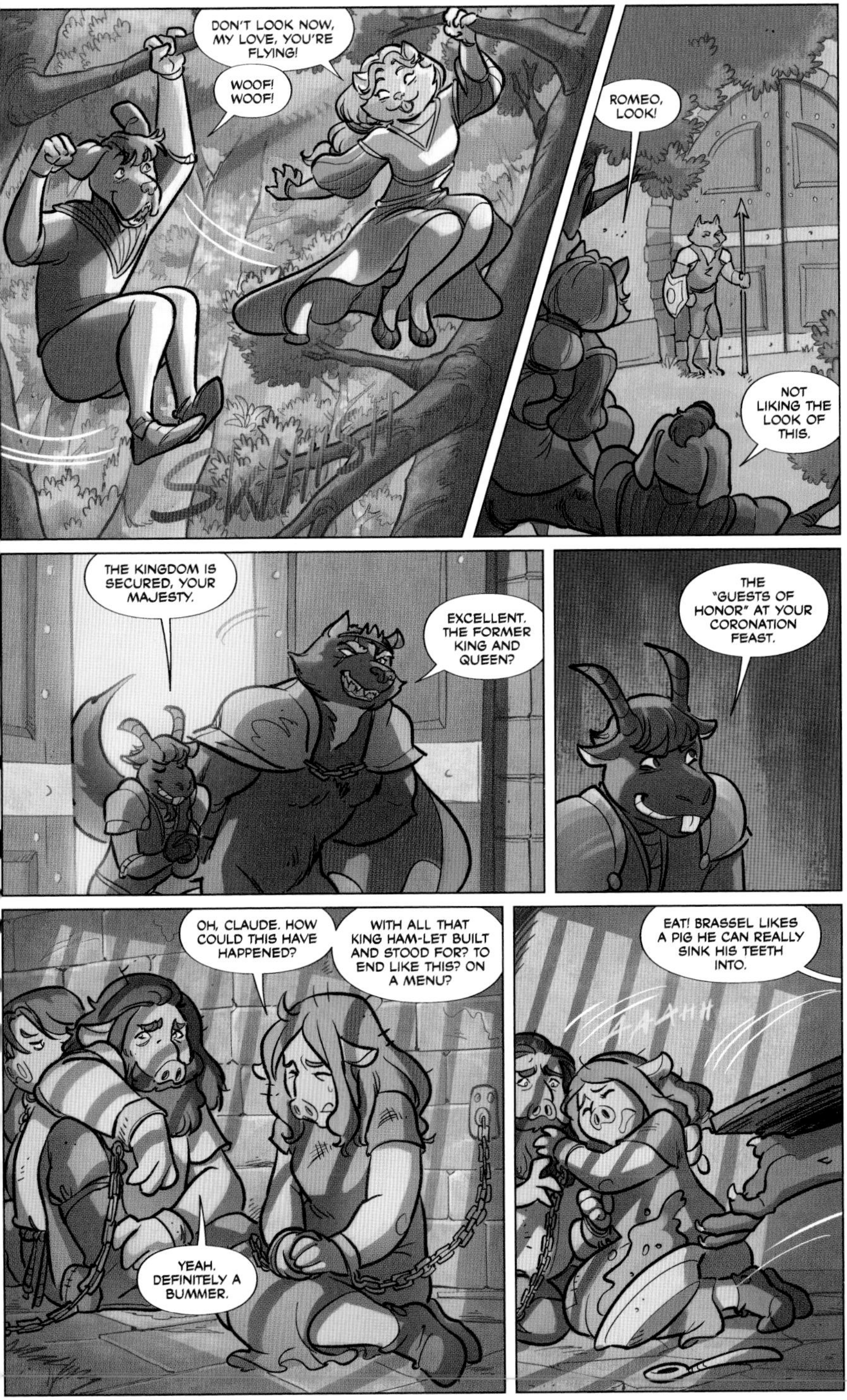
DON'T LOOK NOW, MY LOVE, YOU'RE FLYING!
WOOF! WOOF!
ROMEO, LOOK!
NOT LIKING THE LOOK OF THIS.
THE KINGDOM IS SECURED, YOUR MAJESTY.
EXCELLENT. THE FORMER KING AND QUEEN?
THE "GUESTS OF HONOR" AT YOUR CORONATION FEAST.
OH, CLAUDE. HOW COULD THIS HAVE HAPPENED?
WITH ALL THAT KING HAM-LET BUILT AND STOOD FOR? TO END LIKE THIS? ON A MENU?
YEAH. DEFINITELY A BUMMER.
EAT! BRASSEL LIKES A PIG HE CAN REALLY SINK HIS TEETH INTO.

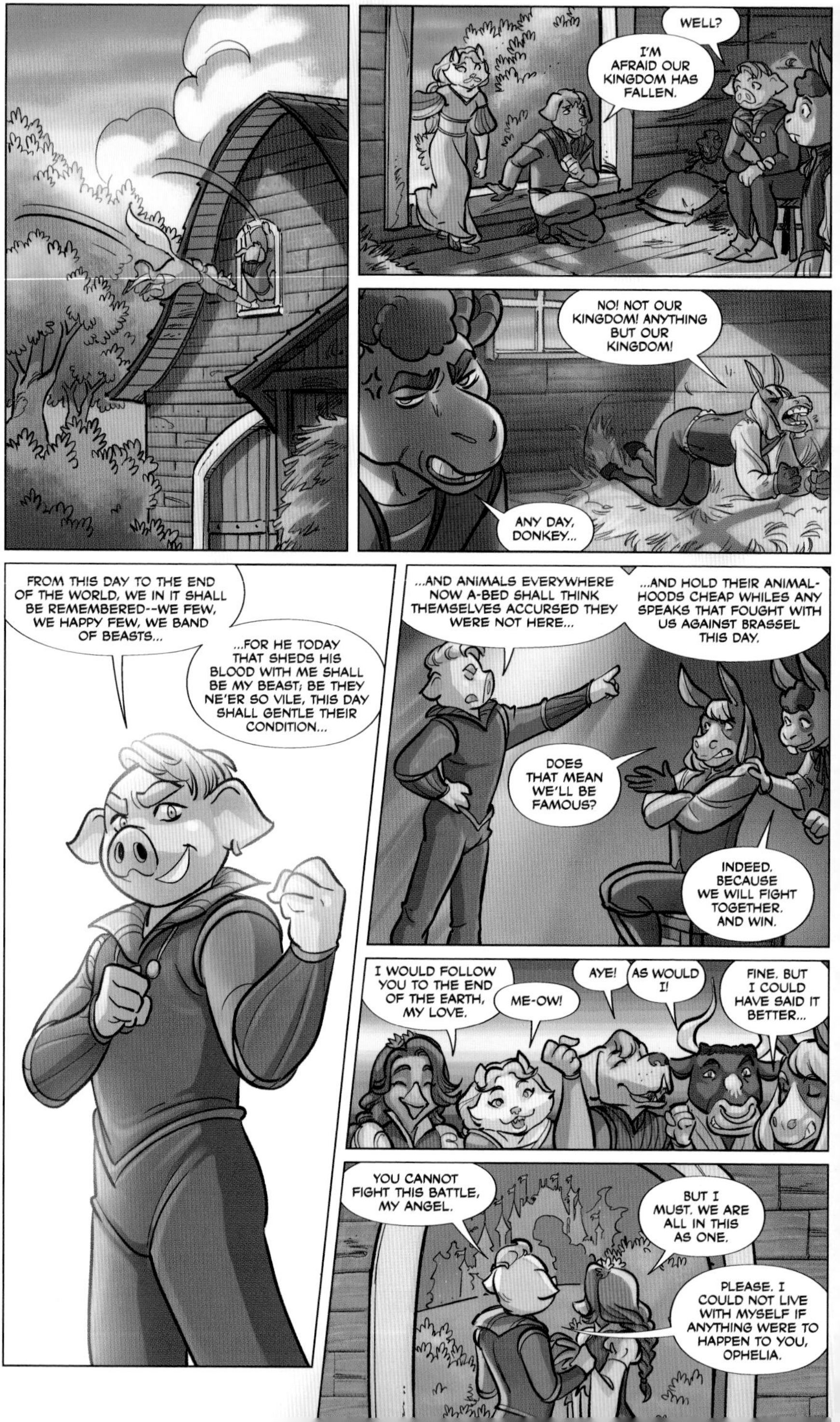
WELL?
I'M AFRAID OUR KINGDOM HAS FALLEN.
NO! NOT OUR KINGDOM! ANYTHING BUT OUR KINGDOM!
ANY DAY, DONKEY...
FROM THIS DAY TO THE END OF THE WORLD, WE IN IT SHALL BE REMEMBERED--WE FEW, WE HAPPY FEW, WE BAND OF BEASTS...
...FOR HE TODAY THAT SHEDS HIS BLOOD WITH ME SHALL BE MY BEAST; BE THEY NE'ER SO VILE, THIS DAY SHALL GENTLE THEIR CONDITION...
...AND ANIMALS EVERYWHERE NOW A-BED SHALL THINK THEMSELVES ACCURSED THEY WERE NOT HERE...
...AND HOLD THEIR ANIMAL-HOODS CHEAP WHILES ANY SPEAKS THAT FOUGHT WITH US AGAINST BRASSEL THIS DAY.
DOES THAT MEAN WE'LL BE FAMOUS?
INDEED, BECAUSE WE WILL FIGHT TOGETHER. AND WIN.
I WOULD FOLLOW YOU TO THE END OF THE EARTH, MY LOVE.
ME-OW!
AYE!
AS WOULD I!
FINE. BUT I COULD HAVE SAID IT BETTER...
YOU CANNOT FIGHT THIS BATTLE, MY ANGEL.
BUT I MUST. WE ARE ALL IN THIS AS ONE.
PLEASE. I COULD NOT LIVE WITH MYSELF IF ANYTHING WERE TO HAPPEN TO YOU, OPHELIA.

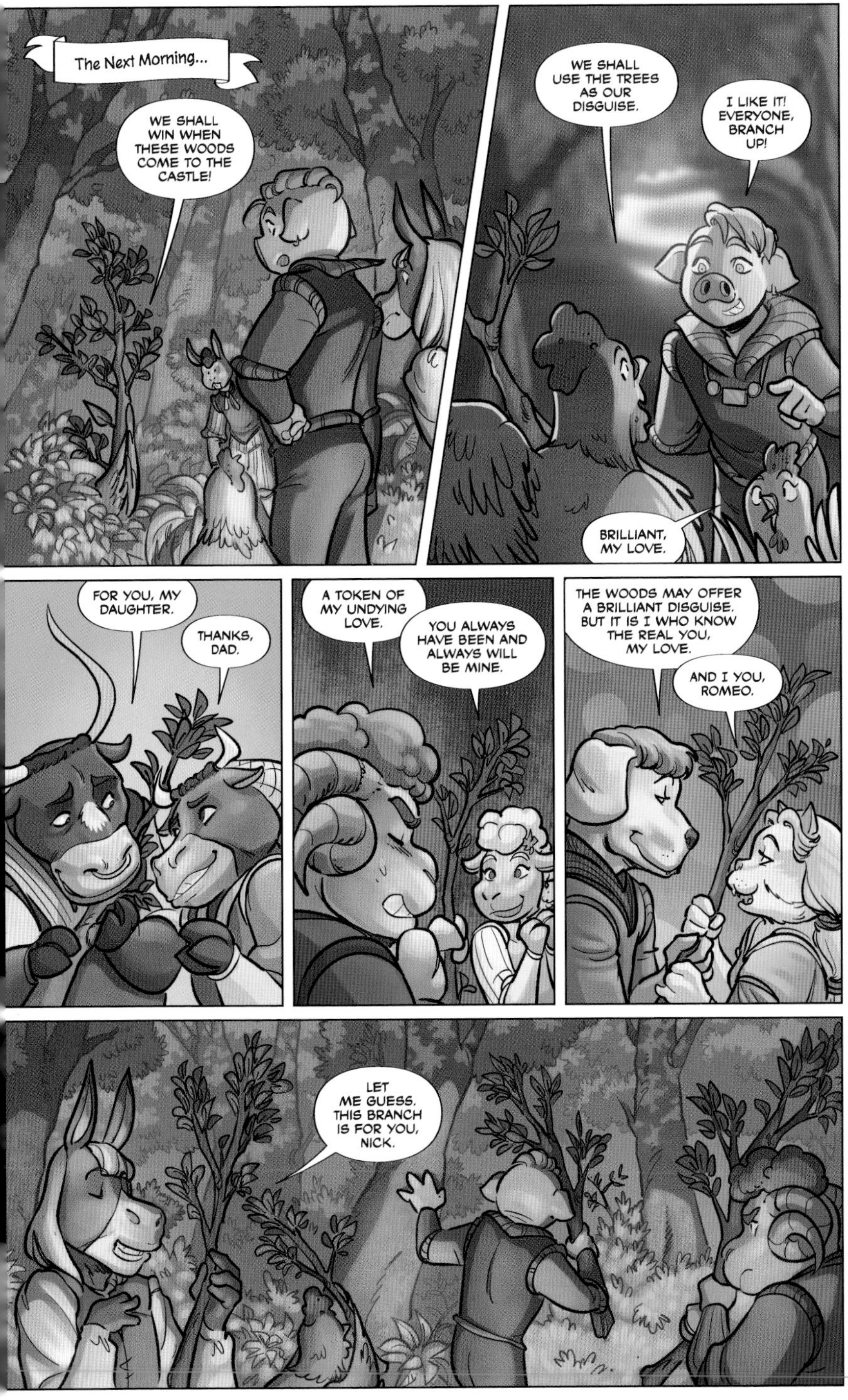

The Next Morning...
WE SHALL WIN WHEN THESE WOODS COME TO THE CASTLE!
WE SHALL USE THE TREES AS OUR DISGUISE.
I LIKE IT! EVERYONE, BRANCH UP!
BRILLIANT, MY LOVE.
FOR YOU, MY DAUGHTER.
THANKS, DAD.
A TOKEN OF MY UNDYING LOVE.
YOU ALWAYS HAVE BEEN AND ALWAYS WILL BE MINE.
THE WOODS MAY OFFER A BRILLIANT DISGUISE. BUT IT IS I WHO KNOW THE REAL YOU, MY LOVE.
AND I YOU, ROMEO.
LET ME GUESS. THIS BRANCH IS FOR YOU, NICK.

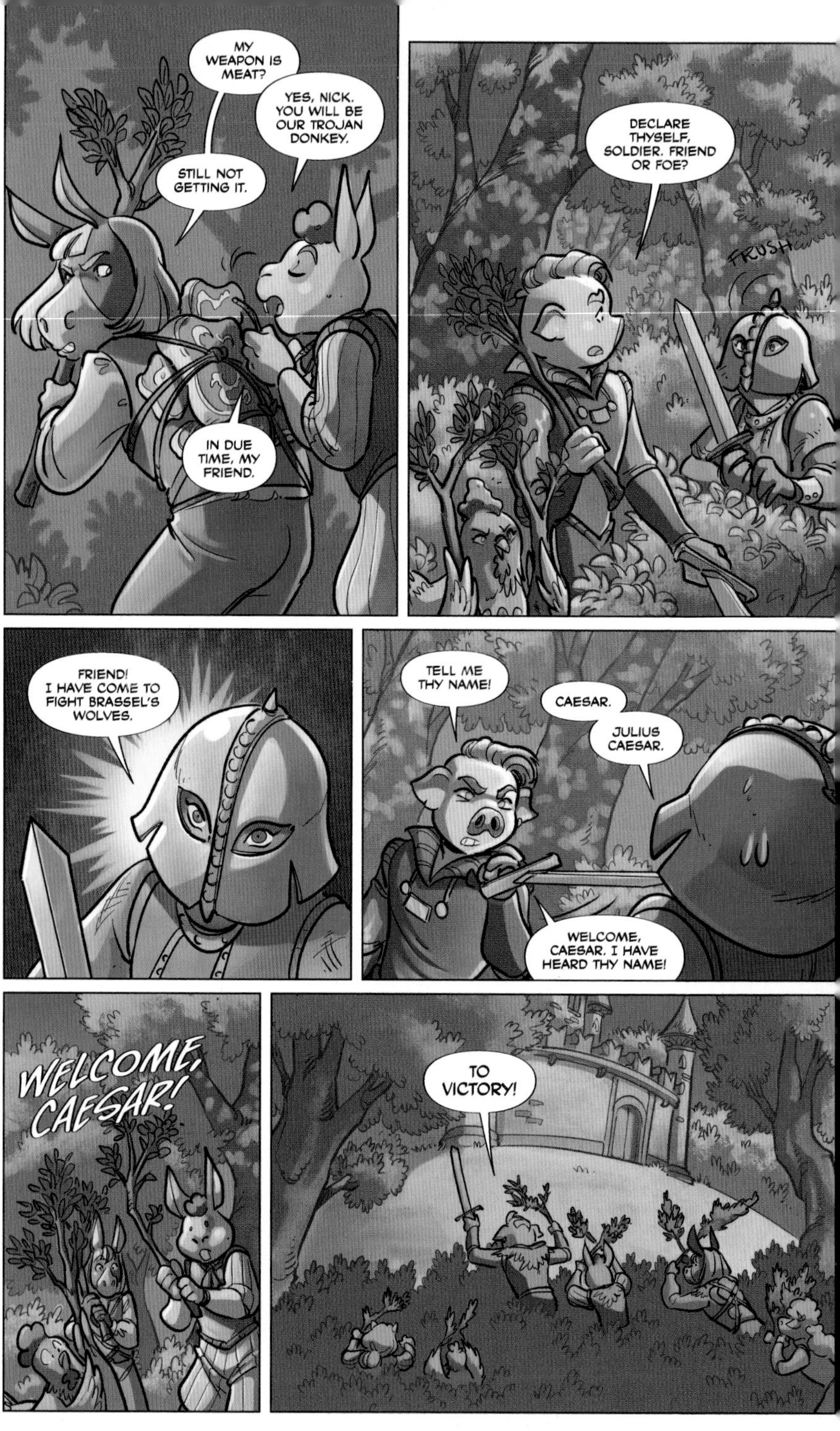
MY WEAPON IS MEAT?
YES, NICK. YOU WILL BE OUR TROJAN DONKEY.
STILL NOT GETTING IT.
IN DUE TIME, MY FRIEND.
DECLARE THYSELF, SOLDIER. FRIEND OR FOE?
FRUSH
FRIEND! I HAVE COME TO FIGHT BRASSEL'S WOLVES.
TELL ME THY NAME!
CAESAR.
JULIUS CAESAR.
WELCOME, CAESAR. I HAVE HEARD THY NAME!
WELCOME, CAESAR!
TO VICTORY!

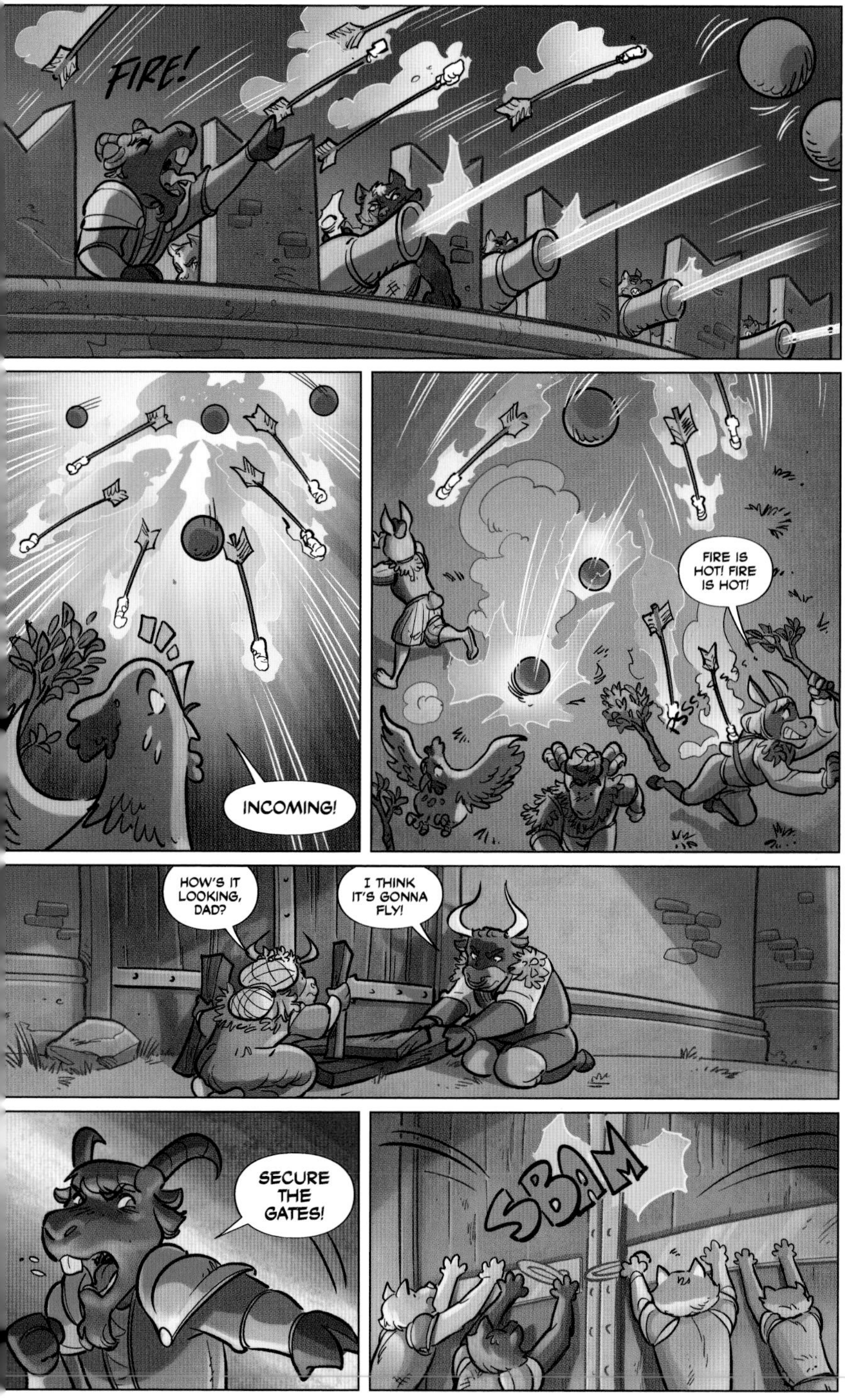
FIRE!
INCOMING!
FIRE IS HOT! FIRE IS HOT!
SSSS
HOW'S IT LOOKING, DAD?
I THINK IT'S GONNA FLY!
SECURE THE GATES!
SBAM

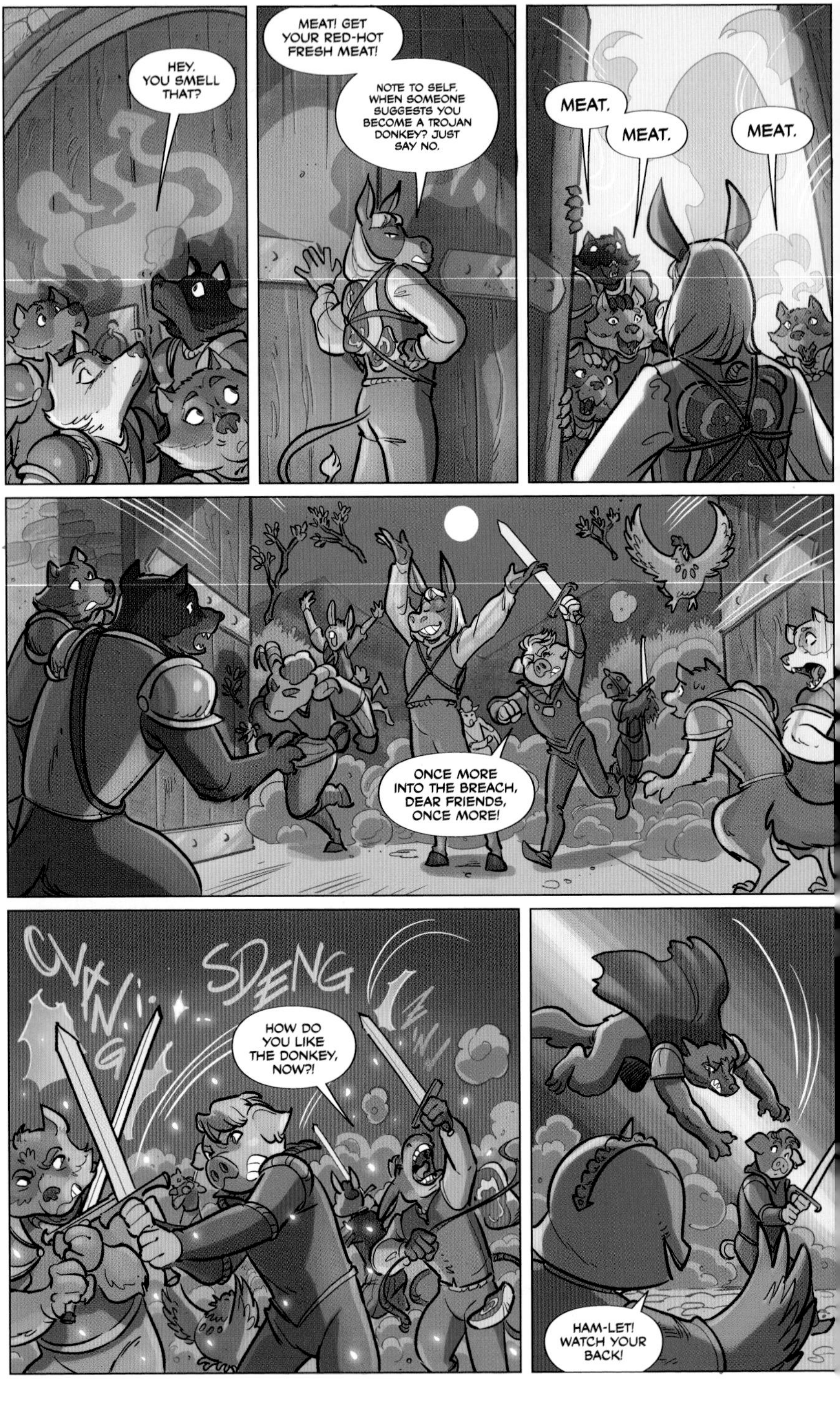
HEY. YOU SMELL THAT?
MEAT! GET YOUR RED-HOT FRESH MEAT!
NOTE TO SELF. WHEN SOMEONE SUGGESTS YOU BECOME A TROJAN DONKEY? JUST SAY NO.
MEAT.
MEAT.
MEAT.
ONCE MORE INTO THE BREACH, DEAR FRIENDS, ONCE MORE!
SDENG
HOW DO YOU LIKE THE DONKEY, NOW?!
HAM-LET! WATCH YOUR BACK!

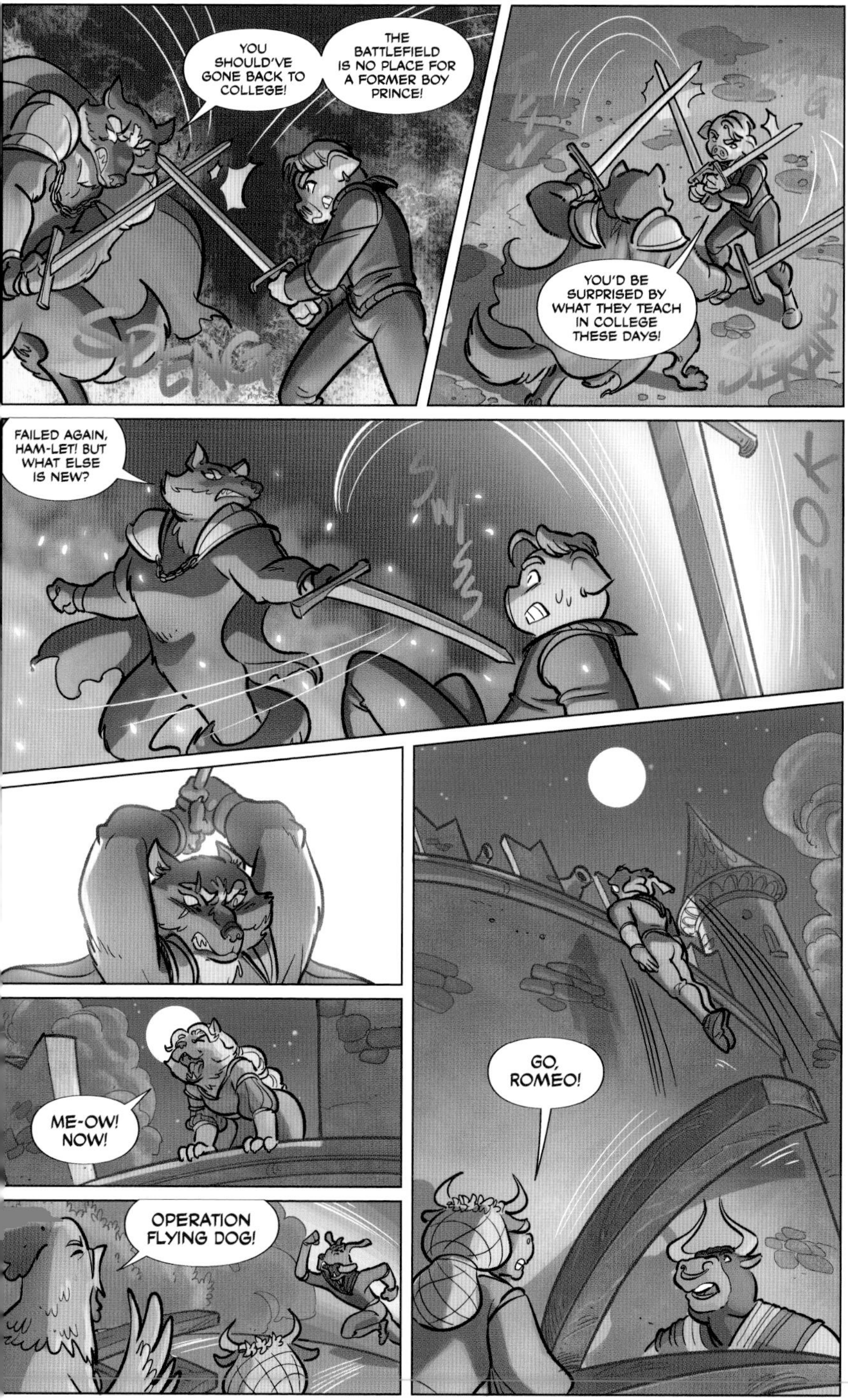
YOU SHOULD'VE GONE BACK TO COLLEGE!
THE BATTLEFIELD IS NO PLACE FOR A FORMER BOY PRINCE!
SDENG
YOU'D BE SURPRISED BY WHAT THEY TEACH IN COLLEGE THESE DAYS!
FAILED AGAIN, HAM-LET! BUT WHAT ELSE IS NEW?
SWISS
KO
ME-OW! NOW!
OPERATION FLYING DOG!
GO, ROMEO!

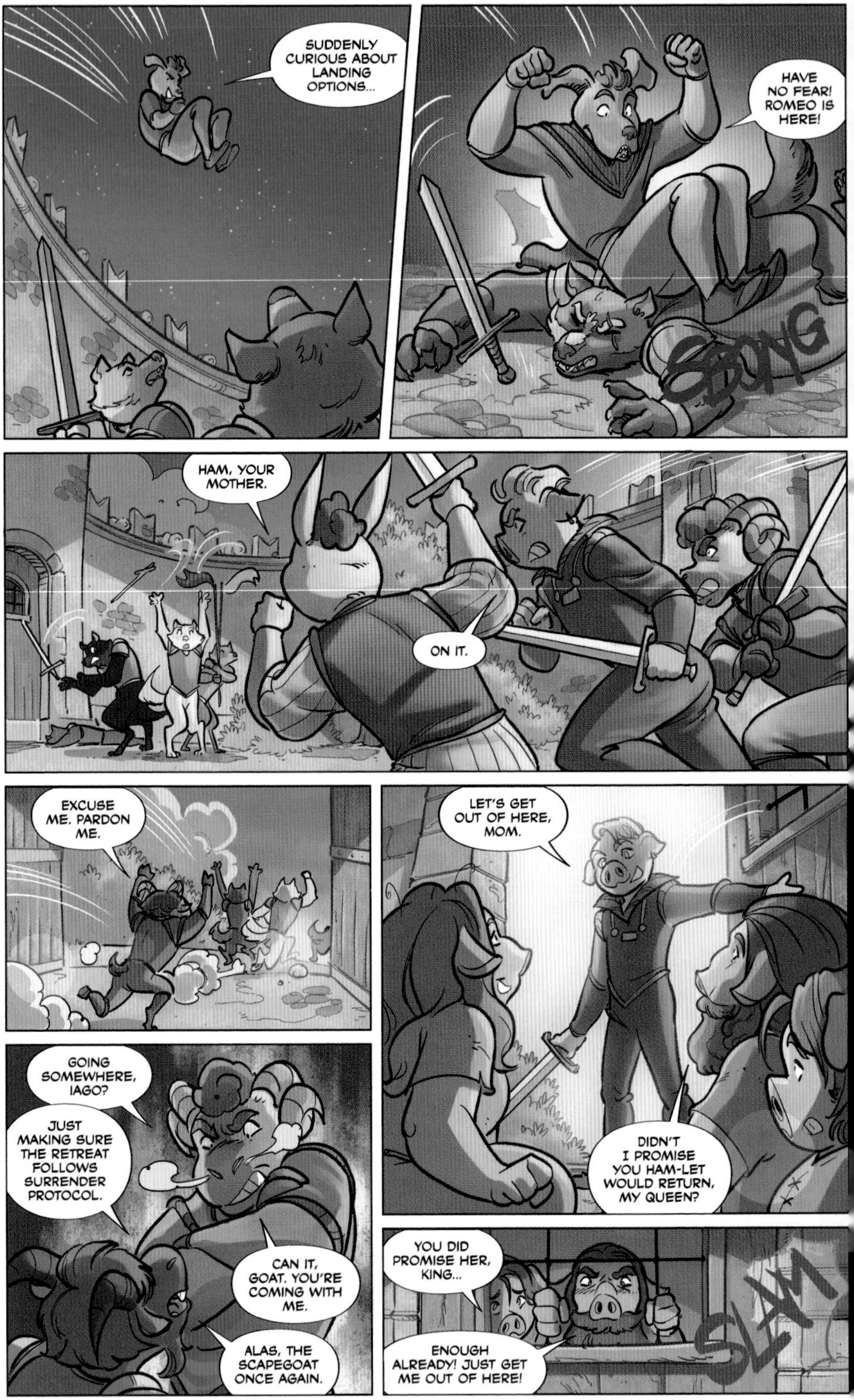
SUDDENLY CURIOUS ABOUT LANDING OPTIONS...
HAVE NO FEAR! ROMEO IS HERE!
SBONG
HAM, YOUR MOTHER.
ON IT.
EXCUSE ME. PARDON ME.
LET'S GET OUT OF HERE, MOM.
DIDN'T I PROMISE YOU HAM-LET WOULD RETURN, MY QUEEN?
GOING SOMEWHERE, IAGO?
JUST MAKING SURE THE RETREAT FOLLOWS SURRENDER PROTOCOL.
CAN IT, GOAT. YOU'RE COMING WITH ME.
ALAS, THE SCAPEGOAT ONCE AGAIN.
YOU DID PROMISE HER, KING...
ENOUGH ALREADY! JUST GET ME OUT OF HERE!
SLAM

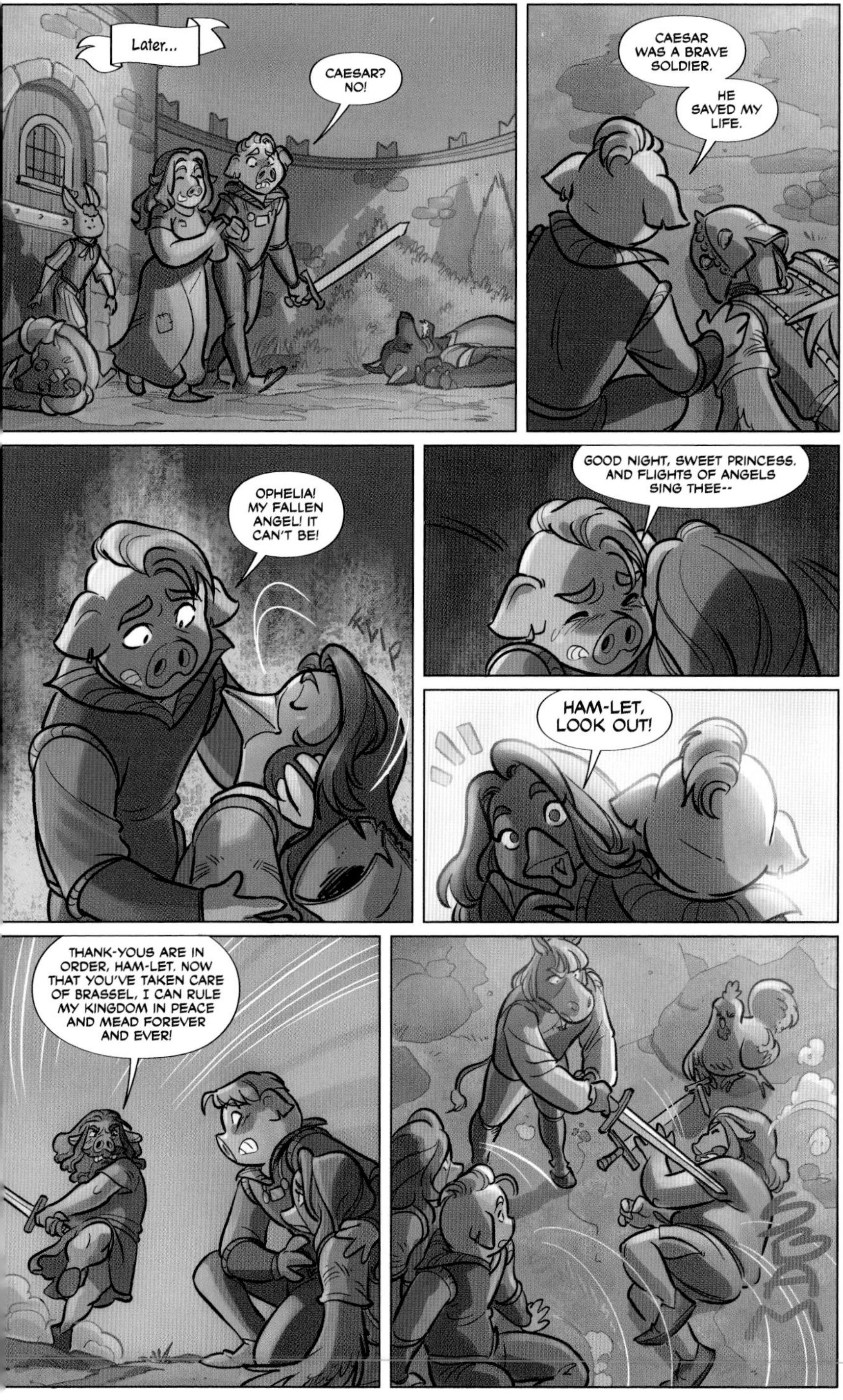
Later...
CAESAR? NO!
CAESAR WAS A BRAVE SOLDIER.
HE SAVED MY LIFE.
OPHELIA! MY FALLEN ANGEL! IT CAN'T BE!
GOOD NIGHT, SWEET PRINCESS, AND FLIGHTS OF ANGELS SING THEE--
HAM-LET, LOOK OUT!
THANK-YOUS ARE IN ORDER, HAM-LET. NOW THAT YOU'VE TAKEN CARE OF BRASSEL, I CAN RULE MY KINGDOM IN PEACE AND MEAD FOREVER AND EVER!

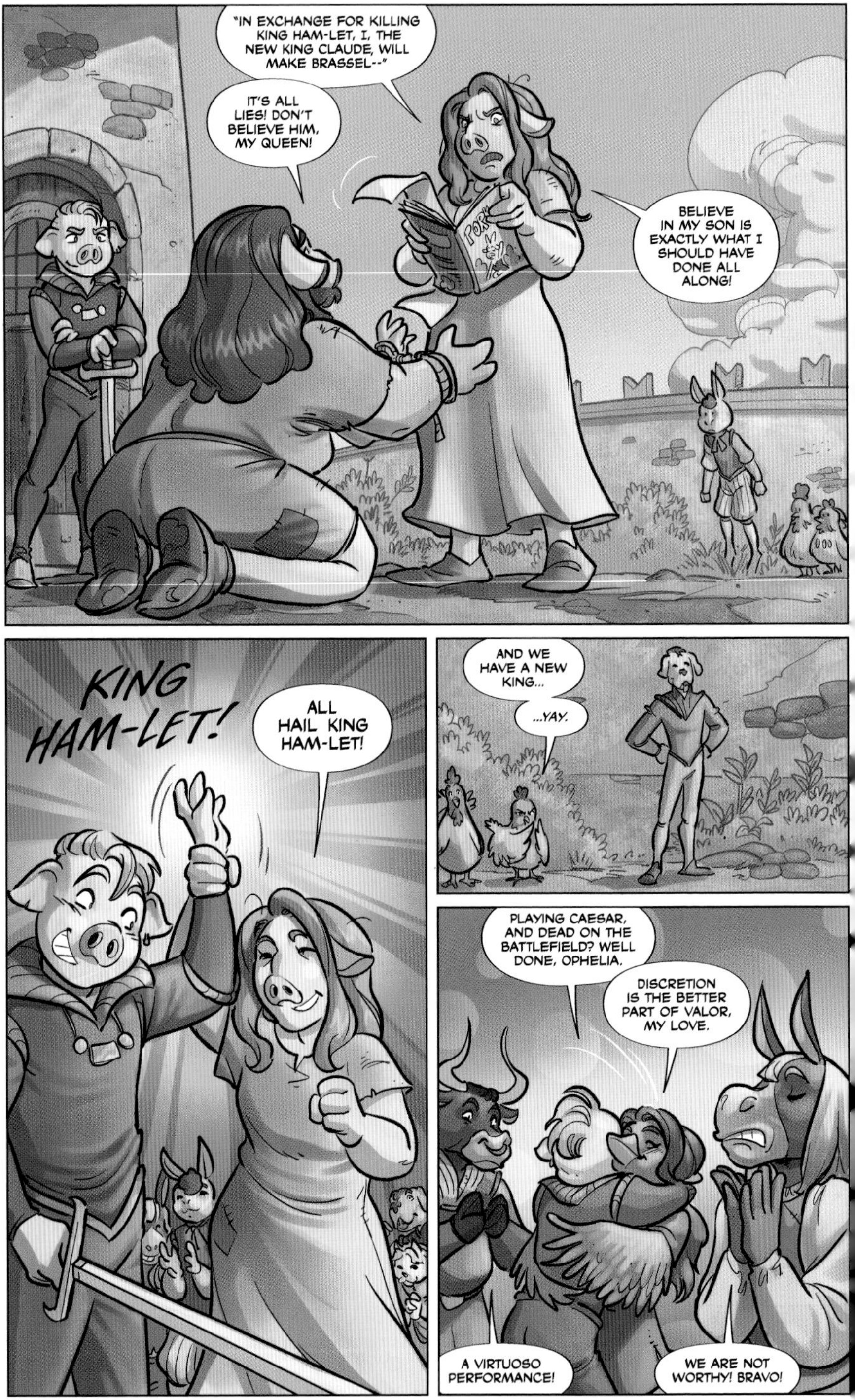
"IN EXCHANGE FOR KILLING KING HAM-LET, I, THE NEW KING CLAUDE, WILL MAKE BRASSEL--"
IT'S ALL LIES! DON'T BELIEVE HIM, MY QUEEN!
BELIEVE IN MY SON IS EXACTLY WHAT I SHOULD HAVE DONE ALL ALONG!
KING HAM-LET!
ALL HAIL KING HAM-LET!
AND WE HAVE A NEW KING...
...YAY.
PLAYING CAESAR, AND DEAD ON THE BATTLEFIELD? WELL DONE, OPHELIA.
DISCRETION IS THE BETTER PART OF VALOR, MY LOVE.
A VIRTUOSO PERFORMANCE!
WE ARE NOT WORTHY! BRAVO!

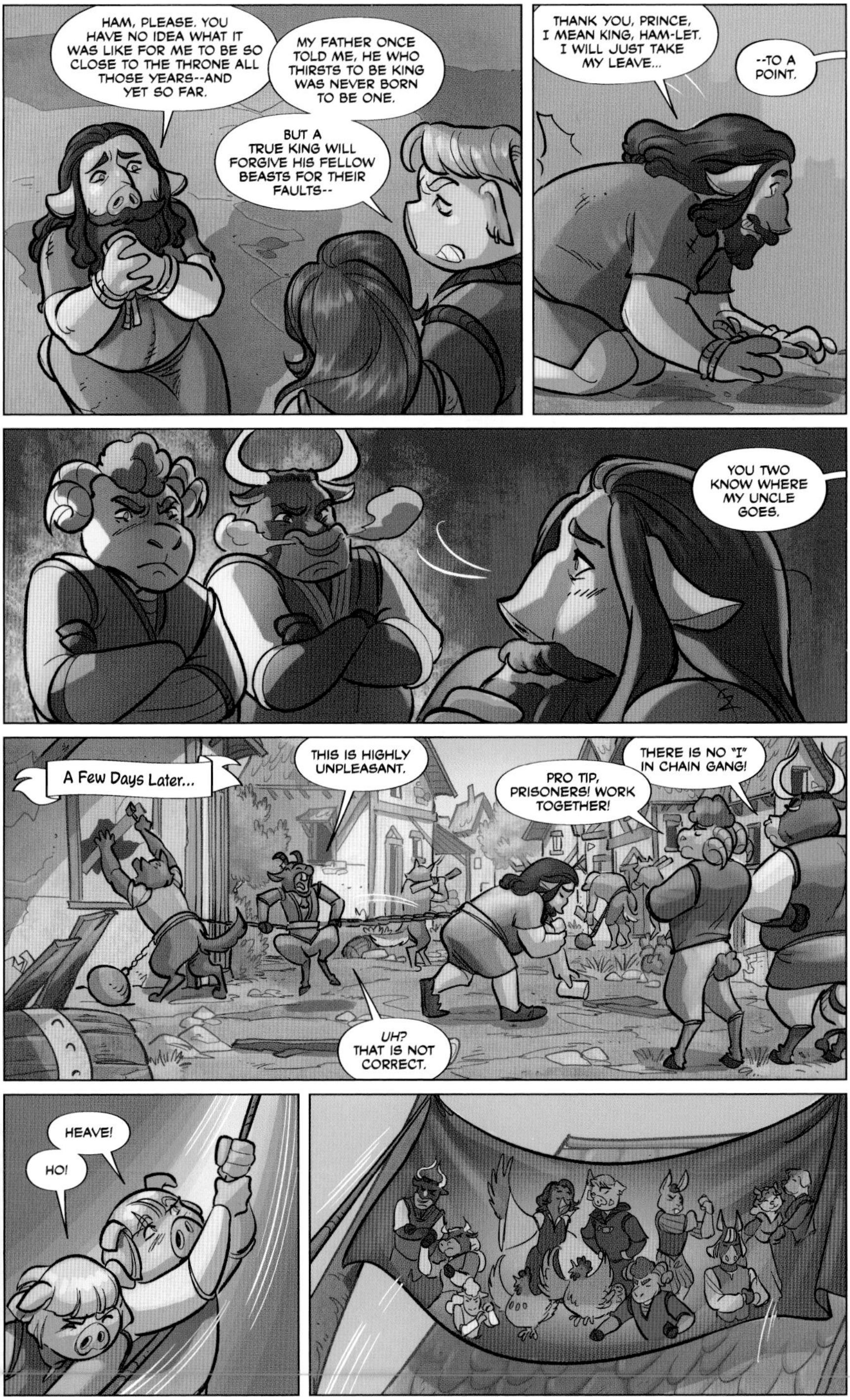

HAM, PLEASE. YOU HAVE NO IDEA WHAT IT WAS LIKE FOR ME TO BE SO CLOSE TO THE THRONE ALL THOSE YEARS--AND YET SO FAR.
MY FATHER ONCE TOLD ME, HE WHO THIRSTS TO BE KING WAS NEVER BORN TO BE ONE.
BUT A TRUE KING WILL FORGIVE HIS FELLOW BEASTS FOR THEIR FAULTS--
THANK YOU, PRINCE, I MEAN KING, HAM-LET. I WILL JUST TAKE MY LEAVE...
--TO A POINT.
YOU TWO KNOW WHERE MY UNCLE GOES.
A Few Days Later...
THIS IS HIGHLY UNPLEASANT.
UH? THAT IS NOT CORRECT.
PRO TIP, PRISONERS! WORK TOGETHER!
THERE IS NO "I" IN CHAIN GANG!
HEAVE!
HO!

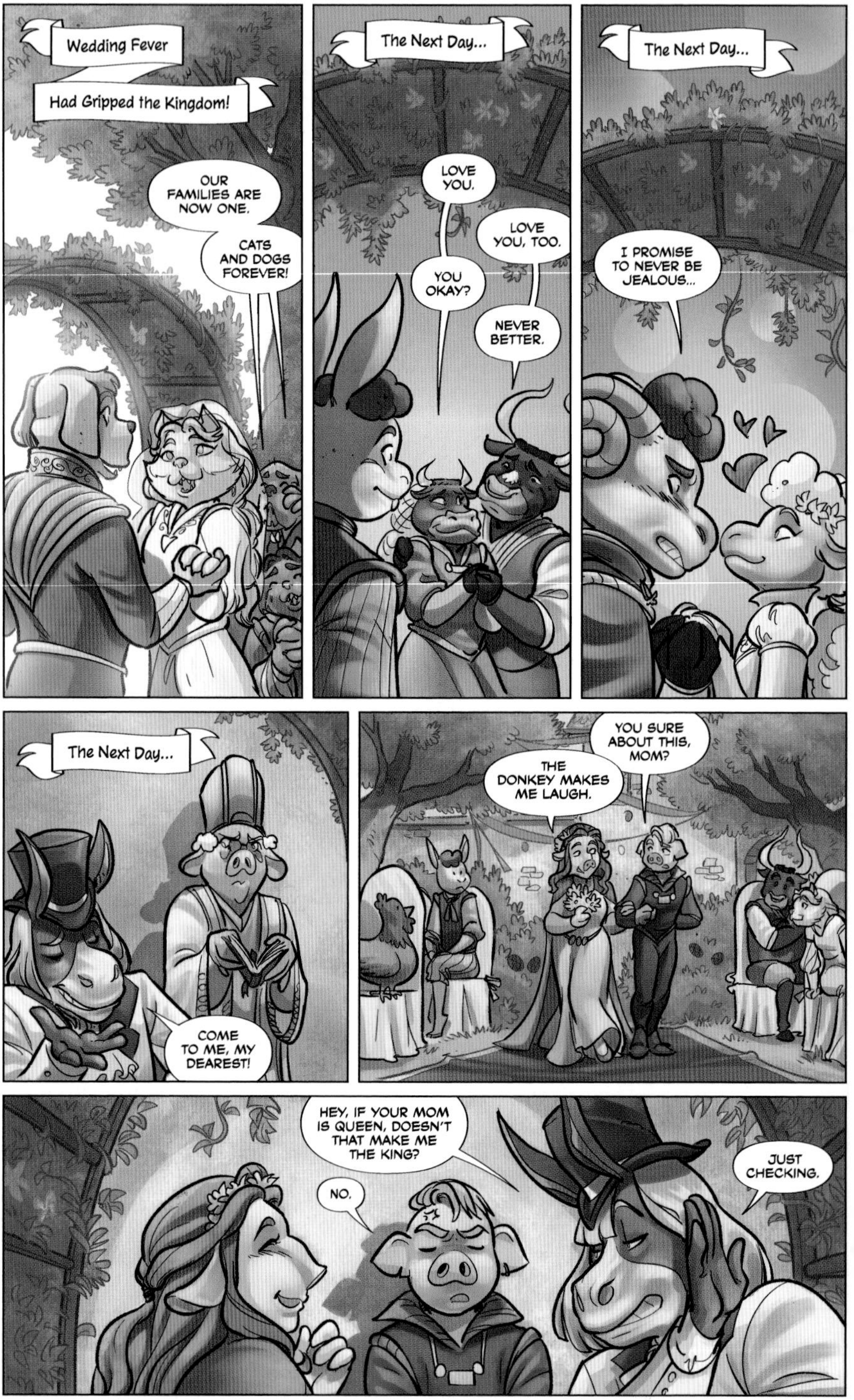
Wedding Fever
Had Gripped the Kingdom!
OUR FAMILIES ARE NOW ONE.
CATS AND DOGS FOREVER!
The Next Day...
LOVE YOU.
LOVE YOU, TOO.
YOU OKAY?
NEVER BETTER.
The Next Day...
I PROMISE TO NEVER BE JEALOUS...
The Next Day...
COME TO ME, MY DEAREST!
YOU SURE ABOUT THIS, MOM?
THE DONKEY MAKES ME LAUGH.
HEY, IF YOUR MOM IS QUEEN, DOESN'T THAT MAKE ME THE KING?
NO.
JUST CHECKING.

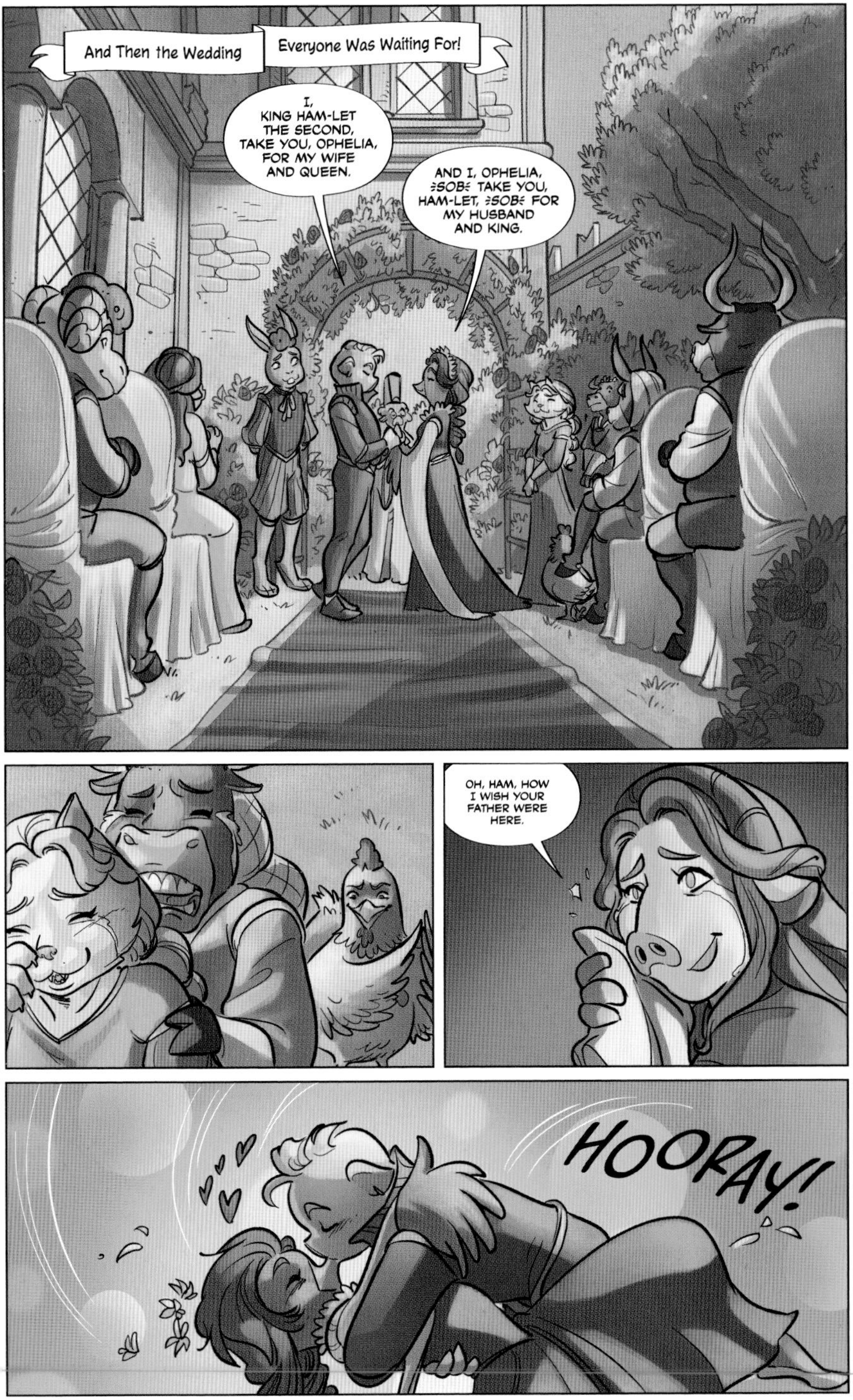
And Then the Wedding
Everyone Was Waiting For!
I, KING HAM-LET THE SECOND, TAKE YOU, OPHELIA, FOR MY WIFE AND QUEEN.
AND I, OPHELIA, ≠SOB≠ TAKE YOU, HAM-LET, ≠SOB≠ FOR MY HUSBAND AND KING.
OH, HAM, HOW I WISH YOUR FATHER WERE HERE.
HOORAY!

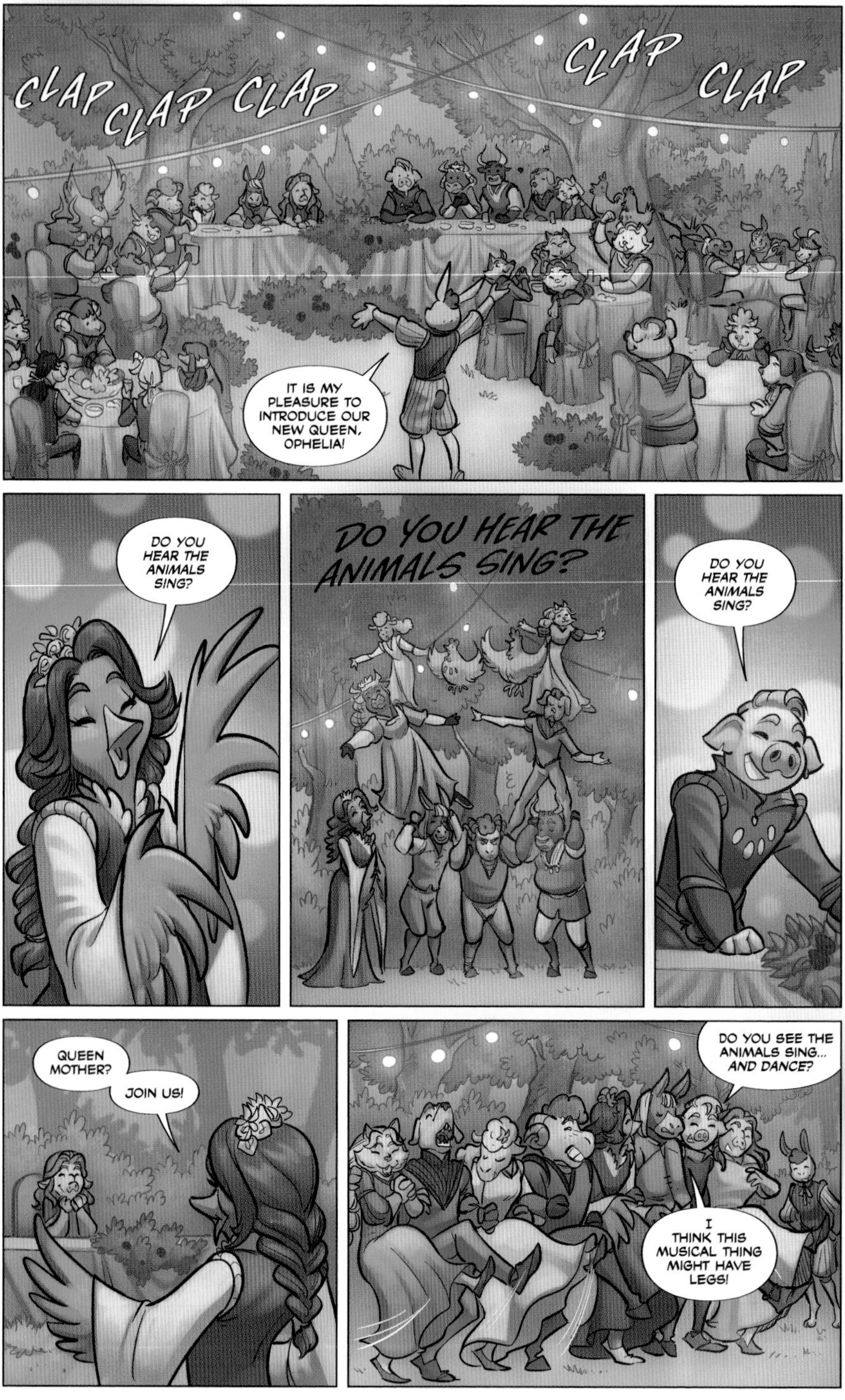
CLAP CLAP CLAP
CLAP CLAP
IT IS MY PLEASURE TO INTRODUCE OUR NEW QUEEN, OPHELIA!
DO YOU HEAR THE ANIMALS SING?
DO YOU HEAR THE ANIMALS SING?
DO YOU HEAR THE ANIMALS SING?
QUEEN MOTHER?
JOIN US!
DO YOU SEE THE ANIMALS SING... AND DANCE?
I THINK THIS MUSICAL THING MIGHT HAVE LEGS!

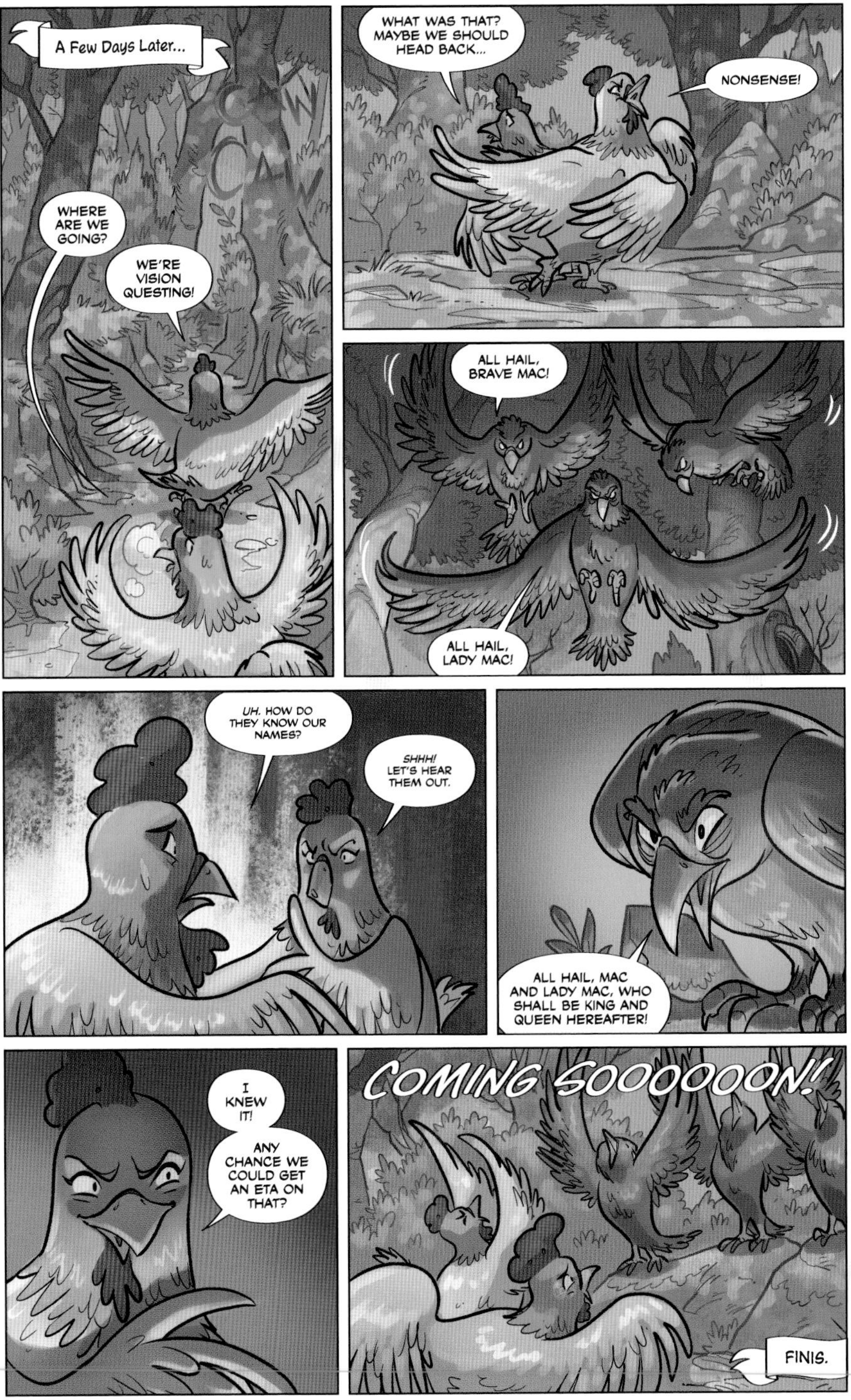
A Few Days Later...
WHERE ARE WE GOING?
WE'RE VISION QUESTING!
WHAT WAS THAT? MAYBE WE SHOULD HEAD BACK...
NONSENSE!
ALL HAIL, BRAVE MAC!
ALL HAIL, LADY MAC!
UH. HOW DO THEY KNOW OUR NAMES?
SHHH! LET'S HEAR THEM OUT.
ALL HAIL, MAC AND LADY MAC, WHO SHALL BE KING AND QUEEN HEREAFTER!
I KNEW IT!
ANY CHANCE WE COULD GET AN ETA ON THAT?
COMING SOOOOOON!
FINIS.

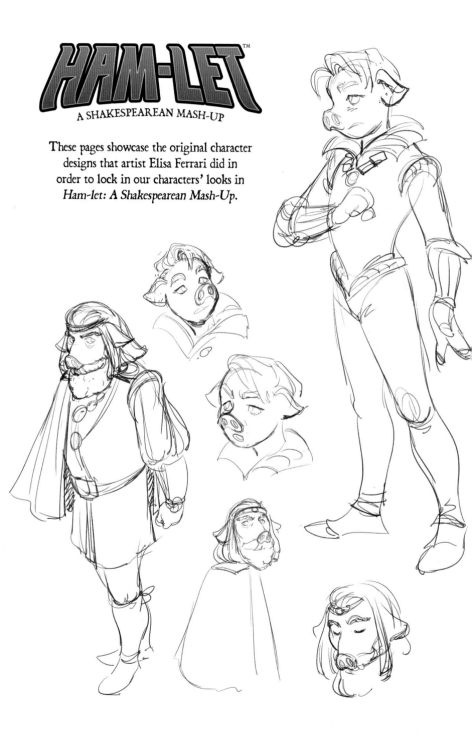

HAM-LET™

A SHAKESPEAREAN MASH-UP

These pages showcase the original character designs that artist Elisa Ferrari did in order to lock in our characters' looks in *Ham-let: A Shakespearean Mash-Up*.

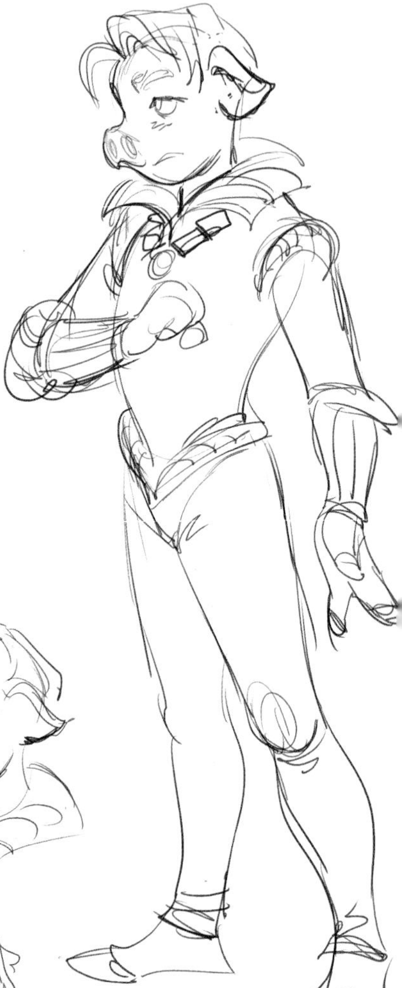

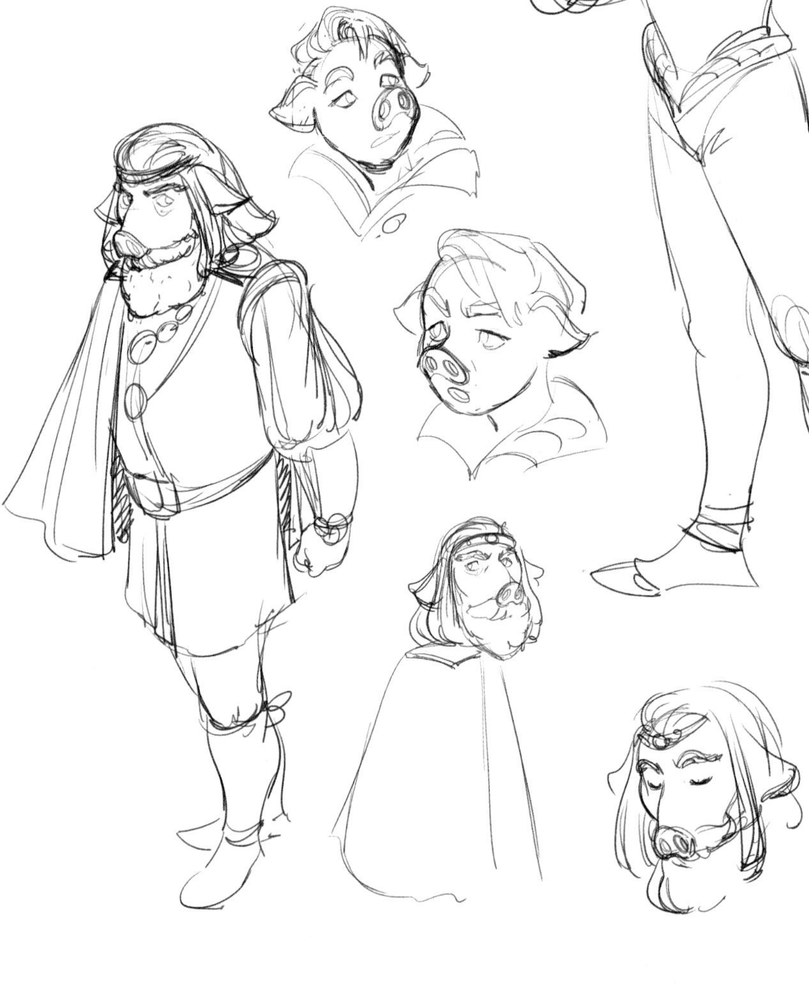

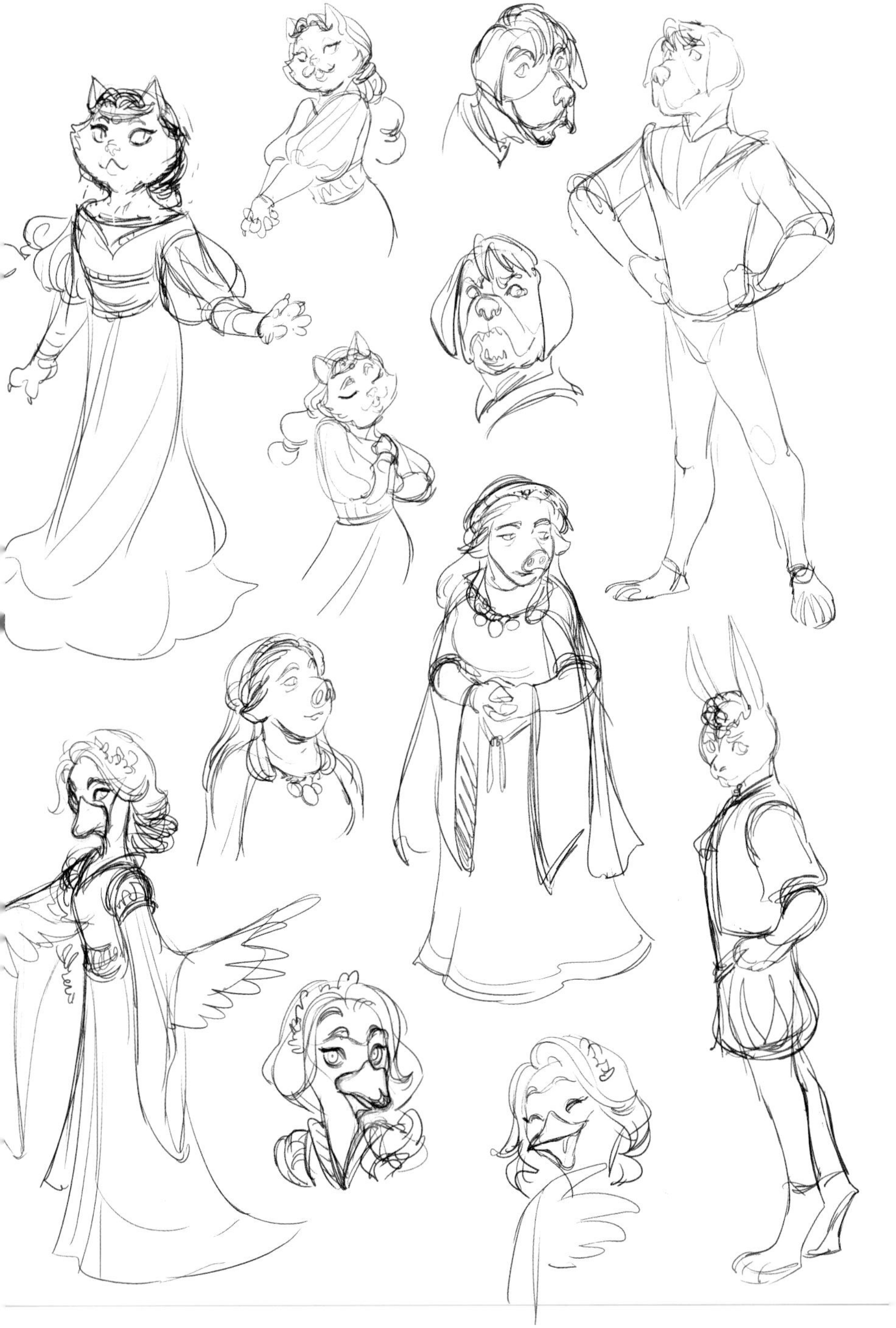

Cover artist Elisa Ferrari's pencils for the front cover art of
Ham-let: A Shakespearean Mash-Up.

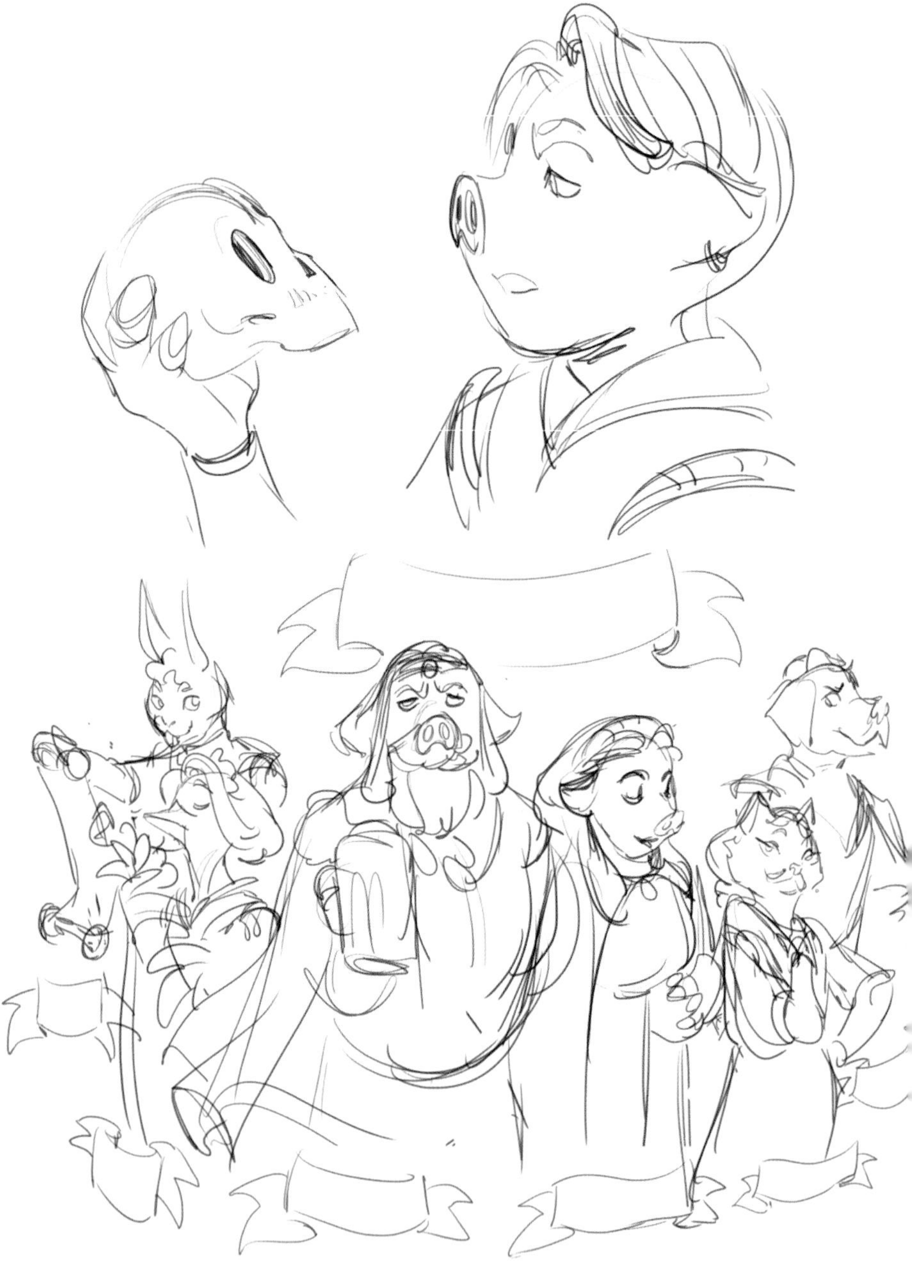

Cover artist Elisa Ferrari's inks for the front cover art of *Ham-let: A Shakespearean Mash-Up.*

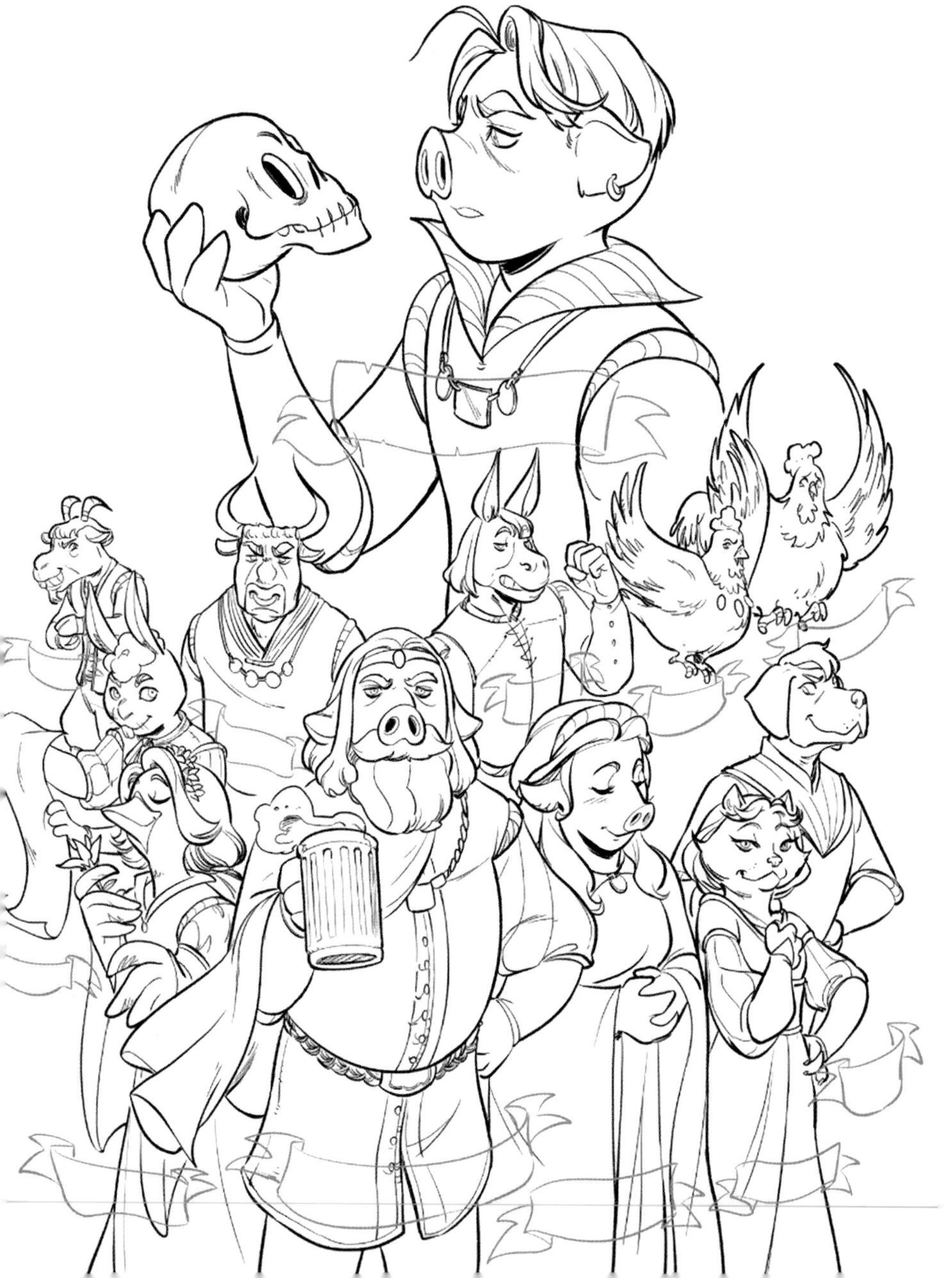